THE CASE OF THE MIX-UP MURDER

DOG DETECTIVE - A BULLDOG ON THE CASE MYSTERY

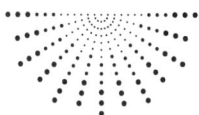

ROSIE SAMS

SWEETBOOKHUB.COM

DOG DETECTIVE - A BULLDOG ON THE CASE

So many of my readers enjoyed meeting Lola Ramsay and Sassy the Lilac Frenchie that I knew I had to write more books with these wonderful characters.

If you missed them you can find the two books with Lola and the introduction to Sassy in my 20 book box set - The Bakers and Bulldogs Collection.

Sassy is modeled on Lila my Lilac French Bulldog. Lila had been returned to her breeder as she was unwanted. At the time, I was looking for an older, small, short-haired dog to rescue. Something I could cuddle, that would keep me company while I was writing. When I met Lila I fell in love with her and that as they say, was that.

Can you believe that anyone would not want her? She is the sweetest little bundle of love you could ever meet. Well, someone's loss was my gain. She is a joy to live with, though she does like to pinch my socks. Nothing makes her happier than getting out of bed and pinching my socks. It has become such a joke that I put a pair on the bed just for her.

Now, all I needed was a new name and so I asked you, my wonderful readers, to come up with a name. There were some great ideas but the one that suited the character the most was Sassy Pants by Sandra H. Thank you, Sandra, we love the name.

I'm so pleased that my wonderful cover designer has managed to bring photos of Lila/Sassy to life for the covers. Much of what Sassy does comes from Lila, you will have to decide if I can hear her talking. 😊 I hate to admit this, but I talk to her constantly.

Read on for my next book, where Sassy and Lola have relocated to a sleepy British village to stay with a friend. I hope you enjoy it.

Join my newsletter at SweetBookHub.com to grab a FREE copy of Smudge and the Stolen Puppies FREE here

Sweet books you will love to read and can share with all the family.

If you missed the first book you can grab it here

A SLEEPY ENGLISH VILLAGE

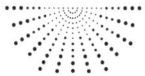

It was three years since Lola's head injury. Recovery had been difficult, almost as difficult as the guilt of survival, and then something strange happened.

Lola had started to hear the voices of animals.

It was mainly dogs, sometimes the odd cat, and once or twice a horse. At first, she thought she was losing her mind — what else could it be? But with time, she grew to accept it. Which led to this exact moment, her looking down at her little French Bulldog sitting on the pavement staring up at her.

"Sad," the dog spoke into her mind.

"What's wrong, Sassy?"

The dog shook, her pale greyish brown coat shimmering in the afternoon sun. In this light, her coat almost looked lilac, and her eyes were pieces of precious amber. Love was reflected in those eyes and the dog's mouth was open in a smile as big as her personality. A pink tongue peeked through purple lips and Lola felt her love which let her anxiety melt away.

"Not me," Sassy said. "You."

A bang broke the idyllic peace of the British village, and for a moment Lola was back in the aftermath of an IED explosion. It was hard to breathe in the dry Afghanistan air.

The Frenchie pawed against her leg. It was enough to pull her away from the past and away from the memory of losing most of her platoon. This was England and she was safe. It was simply a car backfiring, nothing to worry about.

"Sad?" Sassy repeated.

"Not really sad," Lola said and continued walking up the hill towards the shop. "I love it here, and I know Tanya is happy to have us, but things are heating up between her and Wayne, and I feel..."

"Like a cat at the dog park," Sassy said in her mind.

Lola chuckled. "Well, maybe not exactly as bad as that, but at times I want to give them their space."

Sassy had been through enough problems of her own: abandoned, beaten, and starved. From the first moment Lola had seen her, she had felt a connection with the pup. And Sassy, for her part, had helped Lola accept this gift or curse whatever it may be.

But neither of them were prepared for what was about to come.

"Don't mind walking."

Lola bent down and scratched Sassy behind her ears. The little Frenchie grumbled in appreciation and looked up adoringly. As the scratch continued she closed her amber eyes and rubbed her head against Lola's hand.

The roar of a big engine startled Lola and she stood, turning to see a grey Mercedes coming up the hill toward her. There was nothing sinister about it, the village was just so quiet that you could almost forget that cars existed. The noise had set her pulse racing and for a moment she returned to the horrors of war.

"You okay?" Sassy's voice was clear in Lola's head.

"Yes, I'm good." Lola let out a sigh of relief as the closeness of the dog brought her back to the present. "Let's go get that milk."

The sound of Tanya Buchanan, and her police detective boyfriend, Wayne Foster, being friendly in the bedroom had been the main reason for her coming out for a walk this morning. Her excuse, not that she needed one, or that her friends would even know she was gone, was to get a pint of milk from the local shop. It was just a short walk, 10 or 15 minutes; after all, the village only had a few streets. It was nice to get out and visiting the shop was a good enough reason, she had been meaning to call in for some time now. The owner was said to be quite a character.

They continued up the hill along the street called The Edge. Most of the houses were magnificent, not all big, but beautifully maintained with fabulous views as had Tanya's.

Lola Ramsey strolled down the quiet street listening to the songs of the birds singing in the treetops. The sun warmed her back and she pushed a lock of long black hair over her ear as a gentle wind had teased it out of her ponytail.

On either side of her, thatched cottages sat back from the road; just a few weeks ago she couldn't keep her eyes off them. South-Brooke was a tiny village close to the city of Lincoln and it was beautiful. Picture postcard beautiful. The houses sprouted roses and other plants that she had no name for as if they were born together. The plants scented the air so sweetly that she just wanted to keep sniffing in the heady delight, but that wasn't what first fascinated her. The village was famous for its Yew hedges. The perfectly formed and manicured greenery planted in 1880 was famous throughout Lincolnshire and beyond. They were so perfectly kept that they looked to be man-made. An undulating living being lining the streets like a breathing tunnel. She couldn't imagine the time it took to keep them looking so perfect.

The first time she walked past them, she had made the mistake of running her hand over the hedge that looked so smooth. Prickled fingers and a sticky residue told her a different story. Later, the owner had explained that he had trimmed the hedge that morning and it was the sap that stuck to her fingers for long after she had washed her hands.

Roy Patterdale was a lovely man, in his 80's but still so bright and full of energy, though she noticed he held his back occasionally. Like most of the residents of the small village, he had instantly taken to Sassy, Lola's lilac French Bulldog who currently trotted along at her side.

Lola stopped to admire the view out across the countryside. It was magnificent. Like a patchwork quilt of green laid out just for her. Some fields were dotted with cattle, others with horses, others were laid to crops that would feed many this fall; autumn, she thought, as her British friend, Tanya, would say. Though most of the surrounding countryside was flat, this little village and the city behind her were nestled on a hillside.

The local shop was near the top, closer to the road that led into Lincoln. This would be the first time that they had been in it, and Lola realized she had forgotten to put on Sassy's service jacket. Her Frenchie was a fully trained service dog helping her to cope with her attacks of PTSD. She had an official jacket that allowed her access into shops and other establishments, but Lola had been tired this morning and completely overlooked the need to put it on.

For a moment, she thought about heading back. There had been some worrying stories on the local news about dogs being stolen. French Bulldogs were especially prone to theft. They had become very popular, and very expensive to buy. There was no way Lola was leaving her little friend outside the shop.

"Will let me in," Sassy said.

"We will see, if not we will just walk back," Lola said.

There were no words in reply just a feeling of love that filled Lola's mind. It was something the Frenchie was very, very good at. It bolstered Lola and made her feel she could face anything.

Up ahead, she saw the shop. It looked a little out of place in the immaculate village. A bright red banner said 'Tilly's,' and the opening hours of seven till seven. Taking a breath, Lola pushed open the door and almost jumped as a bell jangled above her.

"Calm," the voice said in her mind.

"I'm good," she mumbled hoping no one would hear her.

"Oh, my, it is so good to finally meet you. I'm Tilly, Tilly Trotter."

Lola looked up into a pair of shrewd brown eyes surrounded by circular glasses that made the woman look a little bit like a mole peering out at her. Lola almost expected her nose to twitch. Her hair was grey, short, and practical, her nose small, her skin pale as if she spent much of her time out of the sun. Lola heard Sassy chuckle and she made little grunting noises. "Mole," was loud and clear in her mind but there was no malice in the teasing. Lola looked back at the shopkeeper, and those eyes seemed to see right through her.

"To meet me?" Lola managed.

The woman in front of her smiled and it was as if the sun came out. There was no judgment, just a feeling of welcome.

"Lady smell nice," Sassy said in Lola's mind. Lola understood it did not mean that she smelt sweet or fragrant or even of chicken, one of Sassy's favorites, but that she smelt like a good person. Lola didn't understand how the Frenchie knew, but she did. Somehow, she could scent out people's emotions and sometimes whether they were good or bad. It was a handy skill for a detective, but not all of those Sassy thought were bad people, did bad things.

"I'm not the famous Tilly Trotter. I think I was born before she was even thought about. Who knows, perhaps Catherine Cookson named her after me!" Tilly smiled and crinkled up her eyes making her look even more like a mole.

Lola bit back a chuckle, Tanya had warned her that the shopkeeper was lovely but a tad eccentric and that she was named the same as a famous character in some British novels and a drama series. She had bet Lola that Tilly would mention it within a minute of their meeting. It had been seconds.

"It is so good to meet you." Tilly stuck out her hand and Lola took it. The hand was so small and a little bony but her grip was firm and confident.

"You too," Lola said still a little taken aback and wondering what the shopkeeper knew about her.

"I hear you're a lady Private Investigator from America? I know Tanya so well, have known her since she was a baby, and have been dying to meet you. It must be such an exciting life solving all those crimes. All I do is stay here behind the counter, it's very boring."

It seemed that Tilly knew so much about her but she seemed friendly enough and so Lola offered her a smile. "Yes, that's right."

Tilly bent down and stroked Sassy's head. "And you must be Sassy, I've heard so much about you too. You're a clever little dog who helps your mum out. Well, you're always welcome in my shop."

A sense of relief washed over Lola. At least she knew it wouldn't matter if she left the jacket behind in the future. On the floor, Sassy rolled onto her back and Tilly was giggling as she rubbed her soft pink tummy. The Frenchie's tongue lolled out of her purplish lips and her paws were waving in the air. It seemed that the two of them were friends already.

"Well, I better get some work done," Tilly said, standing up remarkably easy for a woman of her age and walking back behind the counter. "Was there something I can get for you?" she asked, looking at Lola.

"I came in for some milk, but I'll have a quick glance around," Lola said and began to wander down the narrow aisles of the shop. It was small, but surprisingly well-stocked and had everything from stationery to children's toys, to food and staple items. In the fridge, Lola picked out her milk and then spotted some croissants on the shelves next to the fridge. She thought they would be nice for breakfast. Grabbing those as well she wandered down the next aisle.

The jingling of the doorbell didn't startle her this time as another customer came in. It was a tall and broad man dressed in a checked shirt and working trousers. A wool hat covered his hair and his skin was tanned deeply. She had seen the man driving a huge green tractor around the village on several occasions. He nodded at her and then walked to the selection of cookies... biscuits..., Lola corrected her terminology to the British and wondered if she would ever get used to it.

The man was now at the counter. "Morning, Tilly, have you heard about Fred Johnson?" he asked.

"No, is he all right?"

The man shook his head and for some reason, Lola got a feeling of dread. This was such a quiet little village and since she opened her private investigations business all she got was divorce cases from the nearby city and one missing cat. It looked like her work would be mainly spousal cheating. It was depressing. In fact, this morning she was going to meet another woman who believed that her husband was playing around.

Of course, she didn't want there to be a murder every day but she was finding these cases a little bit tedious. Maybe it was because she was a romantic at heart and chasing down all these cheats was destroying her belief in love.

"Wayne, Tanya," the words were said in her mind and Lola knew that Sassy was reminding her that her friends were very much in love and very loyal to each other. "Melody, Alvin," Sassy continued. Melody and Alvin Hennessey were good friends from back in Port Warren in the USA. Along with their super cute little French Bulldog, Smudge. They had been instrumental in Lola coming to terms with her gift; well, Melody and Smudge had, Alvin, didn't know. The couple made a great detective team and Alvin, as the local sheriff, was pretty helpful too.

"Thank you," she mumbled before turning her attention back to the conversation at the counter. Inspecting the shelves, she sidled herself a little bit closer so that she could hear them more clearly. It seemed that she was becoming as nosy as Tilly!

"Well, it seems he drowned in that there pool of theirs," the man said.

"Really, Stuart, I can't believe it. He was a good swimmer, how could he have drowned?"

"I've not heard any more. That was it." The man's cheeks turned from brown to a little pink and he pulled his hat down as if covering his ears. Lola realized that he was only in his twenties and it looked like he had a tendency to blush.

"Poor Sandra and the boys. That is just awful. How did you hear?"

Stuart turned even pinker.

"Have you been listening to the police radios again? You know Wayne will have your guts for garters," Tilly said but then she leaned in closer. "Tell me more."

"I swear, I've not heard anything else, but not everybody liked him, you know that. I best go, I'll let you know what I hear." He handed over some money and took his change. "I'll see you soon, Tilly." With that the big man turned and walked out of the shop, touching his finger to his head as he passed Lola.

Grabbing a packet of chocolate chip cookies (biscuits), Lola made her way up to the counter and put her goods down in front of Tilly.

"I hate to speak ill of the dead," Tilly said, "but Stuart's right. Fred was not well-liked. However, he was a really good swimmer. I guess we never know when our time is coming do we?"

"I guess not," Lola said, but as she did so she felt a tingling down her spine and a touch of excitement in her stomach. Could there be a mystery here? No, she was being foolish.

"How are you finding living with the lovebirds?" Tilly asked, her face crinkling up as she grinned. "I don't like to gossip but I imagine it can get difficult."

Lola sighed, pulling her mind away from the drowning she wondered, should she look for somewhere else to live?

A NEW FRIEND

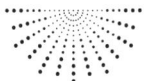

The shop door opened and the bell jangled again announcing the arrival of a new customer. Tilly looked over and waved as an elderly woman with purple hair and stooped shoulders wandered down the aisles.

"Maybe you should look for a place of your own," Tilly said.

"I was just having that very thought, but I wouldn't know where to start. Maybe I should ask Tanya to put me in touch with a local realtor? A recommendation is always the best way to go with these things."

Tilly's face broke into a big smile. "Well, they are called estate agents over here, my lovey, but I might just know the perfect place for you. If you carry on up the hill, just another 10 houses, you will see what used to be the garage. The workshop part was taken down a few years ago, but the property is still there and in good condition. The downstairs was an office with two or three storerooms and a washroom for customers and upstairs is the living quarters. It's nothing special, but it could be made nice and you could use the downstairs to see your clients."

"That sounds perfect," Lola said. "Do you know who I need to contact?"

"Well, it's not on the market just yet," Tilly said with a conspiratorial smile. "I happen to know the owner. I don't like to gossip, but the guy who lived there was not well-liked. If you like the place I can put you in touch with his sister, Alice. She's selling it now that he's gone into a nursing home. I'm sure she'd be happy to talk to you." Tilly handed her a bag with her shopping and the receipt.

"Now, you must tell me more about your exciting business," Tilly said.

Lola wanted to do so; after all, Tilly sounded like the perfect person to drum up some customers for her, but the old lady was approaching the counter. "Why don't I go look at the property and then pop back in a few minutes?"

"That seems perfect. I will see you soon and maybe we can have a cup of tea sometime."

Lola nodded and turned smiling at the new customer who didn't smile in return.

"Good morning, Mrs. Fossdyke," Tilly said in her upbeat voice. "How are the grandchildren?"

As Lola left the shop she could hear Tilly and Mrs. Fossdyke discussing her grandchildren.

Turning right out of the door she continued up the hill until she came to the empty property. It was an impressive looking place with views out over the surrounding countryside but within walking distance of the main road. There was plenty of room for people to park and she could see that the downstairs would convert very nicely into offices for her business. Above that, the property looked roomy enough for there to be plenty of living accommodations. It was also close enough to Tanya's for them to stay in contact. It seemed perfect.

"What do you think?" Lola asked Sassy.

The little bulldog sat staring up at the property, her tiny little snub nose scenting the air. "I smell something," she said and wandered away from Lola. As the lead pulled tight Lola followed. The little dog was sniffing the tarmac. Walking up and down until she found a spot she liked. "Something here," Sassy said.

"What?" Lola asked.

"Not sure, covered by nasty harsh smell, but something. Faint." A bird landed on the gate to the back of the property.

"Bird got to get the bird," Sassy said and pulled in the opposite direction.

Lola laughed as her Frenchie relaxed, the bird had gone and was soon forgotten. "What do you think?" Lola asked again.

"Garden?"

"Of course, let's check around the back," Lola said and together they walked around the back of the house to find a reasonable size garden. Though it was very overgrown it was nicely fenced in and would be ideal for Sassy to run around in. Opening the gate, Lola stepped through, closed it behind her, and then let Sassy off her lead. The little Frenchie tore around the garden for a few minutes as fast as her little legs would carry her.

"Yaaaaayyy," Lola heard in her mind.

Sassy was launching herself at a small black object and she felt her muscles tense. What was it? Was it a bird hiding in the grass? The Frenchie disappeared into the greenery and came out holding a plant pot over her face. She continued to chase through the long grass at full speed and Lola swore she couldn't see where she was going.

The tension had gone. Lola laughed out loud as her little bullet of a bulldog raced around the garden, her head in a plant pot just for the sheer joy of it. You can learn a lot from dogs, they know how to enjoy the moment. How to live for now and to love life to the fullest.

Sassy slowed down, sniffing here and there as she explored. The grass was high and the flower beds were overgrown but there was potential here. Soon Sassy returned to sit in front of Lola.

"What's your verdict?" Lola asked.

"Me like," she said dropping the plant pot between her feet. "Great toys too."

"Okay, then let's go back and talk to Tilly and see what we can find out."

They wandered back to the shop to find Tilly on her own again.

"Good morning, again, the kettle has just boiled," Tilly said.

Lola wasn't sure whether she should accept, but then what harm would it do? Tilly opened the door into the back and took her into a small and rather cluttered kitchen. Though it was tidy and clean there were jars and bottles and tins on every available surface. Only the table was clear and the stove behind it.

Tilly offered her a chair and made 2 cups of tea before offering a treat to Sassy. The Frenchie took it and sat in front of her munching and staring up at her with adoring eyes.

"I think she likes you," Lola said.

"She is adorable," Tilly said. "But, what do you think of the property?"

"It has a lot of potential and Sassy likes the garden." For a moment Lola froze, what would Tilly think of her sounding as if the dog could talk to her?

Tilly smiled. "I thought she would, it's perfect for a dog and there are plenty of places to walk locally." Tilly scribbled some details down on a post-it note and handed them to Lola. "This is Alice's number, she is the one you need to contact. Tell her I sent you. Now, tell me about this business, it must be so exciting hunting down criminals and solving mysteries."

"Unfortunately, most of my cases are cheating spouses or divorce. I have had one missing cat."

"Ahhh, the Simpson girl, I heard about that. Be careful, she will have you looking for that cat every other week."

Lola chuckled for she had thought as much herself.

"Do you have any cases on the go at the moment?" Tilly asked.

"I'm meeting a new potential client at Betty's Tea Room in about a couple of hours," Lola said. "I fear it will be another divorce case but I guess they pay the bills."

"Well, if I hear of anything more exciting I will certainly let you know. I do know Stuart had some farm equipment stolen a few months back, but I think it's all sorted now."

"Thank you," Lola said and got up to leave but before she could walk out the phone rang and Tilly held up a finger stopping her in her tracks as she answered it.

"Hello, Tilly Trotter," she said into the handset, "how can I help you?"

Lola watched as Tilly nodded and spoke, sometimes agreeing or disagreeing with what the caller was saying. There was a little tension around her eyes and it was obvious this was not a good call. Lola wanted to leave, she felt as if she was intruding, but to walk out seemed rude, so she hung on and watched as Sassy went and sat in front of Tilly. The little bulldog had sensed as much as she had.

"I may just know the perfect person for this. You have my deepest condolences. Now, you take care, goodbye, my lovey." Tilly hung up the phone.

"Is everything all right?" Lola asked.

"Well, you heard about Fred Johnson earlier?"

Lola nodded, she remembered something about him having drowned.

"That was his wife, Sandra. The police have put it down as accidental death but she is convinced he was murdered. Now, it might be nothing but perhaps you could call around and see her. Maybe a professional looking into it would put her mind at ease."

"Of course," Lola said but she doubted there was a case. Grief could make you see things and if the police said it was an accident, then surely it was an accident, right?

Tilly handed her a phone number and address and Lola got ready to leave. She just had time to go back for breakfast and then make it to her next appointment.

"I hate to speak ill of the dead but there were many who disliked Fred Johnson. Now, just because you dislike someone doesn't mean you kill them... but it doesn't mean you didn't either."

The bell in the shop tinkled and Lola and Sassy followed Tilly through. At the counter was a man with thick black unruly hair and dark eyes. Lola took in his prominent chin and dimple. The man had a nice smile but he hid it quickly; was he hiding something?

PRINCESS PORTIA

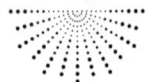

*L*ola stared out of the window as she sipped her coffee. In the garden, Sassy was looking at the neighbor's black cat. The cat sat in a patch of sunshine, licking her paws and looking very regal next to the Frenchie. Sassy sat just a few feet away from her and the two seemed to be staring at each other. It was strange and amusing and also very cute. Lola knew that Sassy wouldn't hurt the cat. The little bulldog would chase rabbits, squirrels, and other little furry creatures but she was always good around cats.

"How are you doing?" Tanya asked, pulling Lola's attention back to the table.

They had finished the croissants and Wayne had left for work about 15 minutes ago. Lola was just having a last coffee before setting off for her appointment.

"I'm doing fine..."

"Are you really?" Tanya's eyebrows were raised beneath a perfectly smooth blonde bob.

Lola felt her hand go to her own hair. Though it was long and straight and needed no styling it caught the wind and she always felt a little untidy next to Tanya. Her friend was lovely but she never seemed to have a hair out of place, she always looked perfect. Lola wondered what to say.

"Yes, I am," she said feeling as if she was being a coward.

"It's okay, we're friends, I understand," Tanya said. "Now tell me what you really feel."

"I just feel as if you and Wayne need some privacy," Lola managed.

"We love having you here," Tanya said.

"I know, and I love being here... but I also think... that... that maybe it's time I looked for my own place."

Tanya's sea-blue eyes were wide above her coffee cup. "Are you sure? You've only been here a few months. Oh, no... are you thinking about returning to the States? I would hate to see you go."

Lola shook her head, but was she? No, England had been good to her. The change of pace, the change of everything was exactly what she needed. Since she had been here her PTSD had reduced significantly. The nightmares were much better too. In fact, she doubted Tanya even knew she was having them. "No, I just think it's time I give you your space and I find somewhere of my own."

Tanya reached out and touched her hand. "Okay, I understand but realize you do not have to. You are welcome to stay here for as long as you wish. That being said, if you do wish to look for somewhere then I will support you."

"Well, as it happens I've already found somewhere that might be suitable. It will need a little bit of work."

Tanya laughed. "That was quick! Maybe I should be insulted?"

Lola chuckled. It was good that they were such good friends that they could discuss this. "No... I was speaking to Tilly at the shop."

Tanya let out a burst of laughter. "I should have known. If anyone knows of a place going it will be Tilly. In fact, let's face it, if anyone knows of anything, it's Tilly."

"I really like her," Lola said as she noticed Sassy coming up the garden. The little Frenchie was trotting, her head high and wagging her little tail behind her. "It's what used to be the garage," Lola said.

Tanya nodded. "That would be perfect for you. It could be lovely upstairs and has the office space downstairs, plenty of parking too. You can have a really good business there and we will still be close enough to drop in for tea. I may let you go, but I still want to see you."

Lola smiled.

"There was some controversy a few years ago, but that's old news."

"Really, what?" Lola asked as the last thing she wanted was skeletons coming back to haunt her.

"It was nothing, just the rough element who worked there, nothing was ever discovered."

Lola breathed a sigh of relief. "That's good."

"I have a class," Tanya said as she got up. "Do you need anything while I'm out? I think we're getting low on milk."

Lola blushed as Tanya opened the fridge. "I got some this morning," Lola said.

"Funny noises," Sassy said in Lola's mind and she had to bite back a chuckle. "I have an appointment anyway," Lola managed.

"I'll just get into something more practical," Tanya said and went to get changed.

"She still be too smart," Sassy said and Lola chuckled. She had to agree, Tanya always looked immaculate when she went to teach her art classes. She always said that she wore old clothes for the classes, ones she didn't mind getting ruined by paints but the little Frenchie had realized that Tanya's scruffy clothes looked better and more fashionable than Lola's Sunday best.

"What were you and the cat up to?" Lola asked.

Sassy huffed and snorted before sitting down and looking up at Lola. There was a serious expression on her face and her bottom lip jutted out a little indignant.

"Princess Portia Ebony Blaze says that dogs are more stupid than cats."

"Oh, well, that's just not true."

Sassy jumped up and spun in a circle before sitting down again in the exact same spot. However, the lip was back in its normal place. "I knew you cleverer than her. Don't even think she's a princess cos she would have a sparkly head thingy."

Lola bit back a chuckle. "A tiara."

"Tiara?" Tanya said as she came through the kitchen to pick up her purse. "Is there something you need to tell me?" There was a twinkle in her eye.

"Oh, no, I was just talking to Sassy." Lola froze, had she really told her friend that she was discussing tiaras with a dog! Maybe she would be leaving the Buchanan residence with her arms secured behind her in a white jacket."

"I swear you and that dog interact in a way I find unfathomable, but it is super cute. See you later, Princess Sassy. Toodles." Tanya threw a wave and left smiling.

Sassy barked, grumbled, jumped in a circle, and then flopped down on the tiles. "If I could be a princess that would show Portia."

"Let me see if I can pick up a tiara," Lola said scrolling on her phone to see what she could find. She had another few minutes before they needed to leave and if they waited just a little longer they would miss the worst of the traffic. "Here, what do you think of this one?"

Sassy reached up to see the offered phone. "Regal," she said with a big smile.

Lola clicked to buy and then grabbed Sassy's service jacket and harness. The Frenchie was trained to help her cope with her PTSD and she had been amazing at it. Able to sense before Lola had an attack and with a touch and a thought she could ground her again. Soon they were in the car and on their way to the appointment.

"Princess Portia teaches me an amazing thing," Sassy said.

"Oh, really, what was that?" Lola asked as she turned the Jeep toward Lincoln and headed for the cathedral district.

"How to always land on your feet when you fall."

Lola could feel the little dog's awe at what the cat had said. Biting back a chuckle she kept her eyes on the road. "How do you do that?"

"You have to be born a cat," Sassy said.

Lola spluttered a little and hoped her little dog wouldn't be offended. She glanced over to see Sassy's ears stretch up just a little further and her muscles all stiffened.

"Sssssquirrel." Strapped into her harness Sassy pushed her squat little nose up to the window and made an exciting grumble come scream that was so cute Lola had to laugh.

"Not funny, it got away and who knows what it will be planning."

"Don't worry, we will keep an eye out for it."

"Good," Sassy said and curled up in her seat to sleep the rest of the journey.

Lola chuckled as she drove along and soon pulled the black Jeep into a parking space near Betty's Tea room and switched off the engine. Sassy was instantly awake.

"You tense," she said.

Lola sighed as she glanced up at the magnificent cathedral to one side of them and the castle on the other. They were like nothing she had ever seen and one day she planned to visit them both. "Not sad," she said. "Just frustrated."

"I understand, you need to sniff more butts, it will make you feel better."

Lola laughed and got out of the car. "Maybe tomorrow. For now, let's go see what Bethany Sharp wants." In her mind, she hoped it wasn't a divorce case. Anything but another cheating spouse!

BETTY'S TEA ROOM

*L*ola unclipped Sassy from her seatbelt and clipped her lead onto her harness. The little bulldog jumped over onto her knee and then as Lola opened the door, she sniffed the air. Lola knew that she would wait there until she was told to get out. It was part of her service dog training and really, a way of keeping her safe. Giving her a quick squeeze, Lola checked the parking lot. As all was clear, she said, "okay."

Sassy jumped out and spun around giving a quick bark to Lola to hurry up. "Adventure," Lola heard in her mind.

"It might be an adventure to you, but for me, it's just work," Lola said a little bit grumpily as she picked up her briefcase and Sassy's service jacket. While she fitted the jacket, which was bright yellow, Sassy wiggled more than usual. "What's wrong?"

"Waste time, why?" Lola heard in her mind and for a moment she didn't understand, but then she did. Sending back a feeling of love, she decided to follow the bulldog's example. What Sassy was trying to tell her was to not waste time on being unhappy. It was a beautiful sunny day, she was in a magnificent city in a foreign country and she had everything she needed. Maybe this meeting would be a boring case but it was a case and she may as well be happy.

"Which way?" Sassy asked as she looked around the parking lot.

Lola picked up her own jacket and checked the map app on her phone. "Down that alley over there." Lola pointed and then blushed a deep crimson as a young couple went past giggling. They had obviously seen her talking to the dog. Lola smiled and shrugged and then set off on her way.

Sassy trotted ahead, sniffing some posts that lined the parking area as they turned onto the street and occasionally stopping to sniff at buildings. "Big dog, bad tummy," Sassy said before trotting on again.

Lola had got used to this; Sassy could tell from the smell on the street a lot about the dogs that had passed this way.

Soon they turned onto Steep Hill. It was a place that Lola loved. A narrow street, cobbles lined the middle but the sidewalk, or should she say, the pavement was easier to walk on. On either side were houses, ancient and amazing, but now turned into quaint tea rooms, shops full of wonderful gifts, and boutiques. Some of them leaned out over the street in a most unusual way.

The climb was tough and there was a railing for people to haul themselves up on and to prevent them from tumbling down.

Sassy trotted on ahead and seemed to hardly notice the punishing gradient of the hill. Lola had read that it was a 16.12° gradient, the fourth steepest street in England. Though she wasn't really sure what the numbers meant she was certainly feeling the climb in her calves. Panting a little she stopped when they reached a place called The Rest.

The seat that had been put there for weary climbers looked so enticing.

"Come on, let's sniff," Sassy said.

Lola took a deep breath and let go of the railing and continued on. She had arranged to meet her client somewhere called Betty's Tea Room. It was just a little further up, nestled just below the square that opened out at the top of the hill. On that square was a magnificent Gothic three-towered cathedral that was once reported to be the tallest building in the world. It was famous for a carving of an imp, known as the Lincoln Imp. Opposite it was an 11th-century Norman castle constructed by William the Conqueror. Tanya had told her all about these magnificent buildings and they planned to visit sometime soon. The castle was built on the remains of a Roman fortress and was one of only two castles that has two moats.

Sassy was pulling ahead and even giving Lola a little bit of an advantage. They made the last 100 meters and there ahead was Betty's Tea Room. It was a charming Tudor building with white walls lined with black sleepers. Little tables were set up outside filled with diners and she could see people inside.

Taking a breath, she did a check; Sassy was wearing her service jacket, she had her briefcase and purse and hopefully, she wasn't too sticky from the climb. Running a hand over her straight black hair she tucked a strand behind her ear and sucked in a breath.

"You great," Sassy said in her mind and she felt a smile cross her face as she was flooded with love.

"Thank you, partner."

"Princess." Sassy did a series of grunts that Lola was sure was a sign of amusement.

They approached the door to see a large middle-aged man with a ramrod-straight back and a black uniform. His hair was dusted with grey but there was something superior about him. Lola watched as he booked in a couple before her and handed them over to a waitress to take to their table.

Clearing her throat she approached the man and cursed herself for feeling so nervous. So he was British, that didn't mean he could look down on her.

"Think he is though," Sassy said with a grunt before she sat at Lola's feet in that way that only Frenchies can. She rocked back on her butt with her back legs stuck out before her and once more her bottom lip was protruding.

"Hi," Lola said. The man turned his gaze from Sassy to Lola and he looked over his glasses at her.

"We don't allow pets in here," he said before picking up a menu and turning away.

Sassy let out a grunt of disgust.

"She's not a pet, she's my service dog," Lola said, trying to keep the panic down though her heart was pounding and she could feel a cold sweat on her forehead. *He's just a waiter, there is no danger here!*

"Really!" He rolled his eyes. "I'm sure you can get those," he pointed at the yellow jacket, "off Amazon, and since when has... such a dog been a service dog?"

Lola swallowed and in front of her, a crash came from over the man's shoulder. Without thinking Lola ducked and grabbed Sassy. Then she realized that one of the waitresses had dropped a tray. It was nothing.

"Calm, all good," Sassy said in her mind and she snuggled up into her face offering warmth and comfort.

"I'll take over, Gerald," came a warm and soothing voice and as Gerald stepped aside Lola saw a small woman who was about 60. She had short grey hair, a kind face, and smiling blue eyes.

"I'm Betty, I apologize for Gerald, he can be a stickler for the rules. You are safe here and your dog is very welcome."

"Lady smells nice," Sassy said as she reached forward and sniffed the air. Lola put her down.

"Thank you, I'm here to meet a woman." Suddenly, the client's name had left her and she lifted her briefcase but before she could open it Betty held up her hand.

"That will be Bethany Price-Williams, she informed me you would be coming. Please follow me." Betty led Lola from the small foyer into another world. The tea room was charming. The tall ceilings were surrounded by ornately decorated coving and the damask-colored walls were covered in artwork of the surrounding countryside including a magnificent picture of the Red Arrows aerial display team flying over what looked like South-Brooke.

Round tables were filled with people and covered with white lace table cloths. The teacups and pots were all china and covered in beautiful and bright flowered designs. Most tables had plateaus of cakes or cakes and sandwiches.

"Yummy in my tummy," Sassy said as she dived forward and grabbed a bit of cake from the floor.

Betty led her to a table and then stood aside. "I will bring you both some fresh tea and you can have a look at the menu," she said before leaving.

Lola gave her a smile and then turned to her client. Bethany Price-Williams was wearing an expression that almost curdled Lola's stomach. Her military training kicked in and she evaluated the woman in an instant. "Mrs. Price-Williams, it is good to meet you," Lola said holding the woman's cold blue eyes but dropping her head to sit before the client could come back with some barb.

Bethany was an aging blonde beauty, expensively and immaculately dressed in a white linen suit and 4-inch heels. Her anger was like a forcefield protecting her from the world and maybe from disappointment. Lola bit down a sigh and raised her eyes. "Now, what can I do for you?" How she hoped this wasn't another cheating partner.

"Lady not happy," Sassy said, and then she curled up on the floor on top of Lola's feet.

"It's about my husband!"

THE STRANGEST CASE

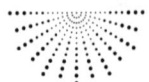

*L*ola sipped her tea and tried to bite back her disappointment. Under the table, Sassy nuzzled her leg before curling up once more. "Please tell me what the problem is," Lola asked.

Bethany raised a perfectly manicured eyebrow and peered over her delicate teacup. Taking the cotton napkin off the table she dabbed at her rose-red lips and then placed the napkin down.

Lola smiled hoping this would disarm the woman who seemed to radiate anger and resentment.

Bethany huffed. "I wanted to discuss my husband, well, my ex-husband. I have a file here for you to look at." Reaching down to her side she retrieved an apricot

Chanel bag and pulled out an apricot folder that matched the bag perfectly, placing it on the table. Her manicured hand was covered in gold rings and she tapped on the folder with an index finger painted to match her lips.

Lola felt herself curl her own fingers into fists. The nails on her hands were short and she struggled to keep them as spotlessly clean as the woman before her no doubt expected. Reaching out to the file, Lola took it but before she opened it she looked up at Bethany. "Why don't you explain it to me first and I will look at the file later?"

For a moment, Bethany's lips narrowed but then she nodded her head and let out a sigh. "I knew what he was like when I married him," she said with anger and bitterness seething out with every word. "After all, I was his secretary and his second wife. I knew he was a womanizer. His first marriage lasted 12 years, funnily enough, that is exactly how long ours lasted too. He's only six years into his new marriage and he comes back to me!" There was a little bit of glee evident in her tight smile.

Lola was getting confused. "Did you say he had come back to you?"

Bethany nodded.

"Then I don't see what you want me for."

Bethany shook her head and sighed, rolling her eyes as if it was all so obvious. "What I want from you is to find out what he is playing at… and then I will make him pay. You see, he came back to me and we have been having an affair for the last three months. A month ago he brought me a key and told me to keep it safe."

"A key!" Lola said.

"Yes, I never did get the settlement I deserved and I wondered if that was what this key was for. Maybe he felt sorry for what he did to me and for the way he treated me. Maybe you can find out what it unlocks and bring me what I deserve?"

Bethany paused to take a sip of her tea only to find her cup was empty. With exaggerated care, she took the milk jug and poured ½ inch of milk into her teacup, and then topped it up with the hot tea. Taking a sip, she leaned back in her chair and then placed the china cup back on its saucer as she continued.

"I really thought things had changed between us. I even wondered if we might get back together permanently but then things changed once more."

Bethany was staring at Lola as if she expected her to understand what that change was.

"What changed?" Lola asked.

Bethany sighed and shook her head. "He became distant and stopped coming around to see me. What I want to know is, is he back with his wife or is he seeing his new secretary? Oh, forgive me for being politically incorrect, they are PAs now, not secretaries. Secretaries was good enough in my day, but not now! I bet she's young, whoever she is. Young, pretty, and probably stupid, as that's the way he likes them."

Lola had to stop her jaw from falling open and bit back a snort. Did Bethany not realize that by insulting his new PA she was also insulting herself? What exactly did she want? "Do you want me to find out if he's cheating on you?" Lola asked, despite the fact that the question seemed ludicrous. This was definitely the strangest case she had ever had. Bethany was cheating with her ex-husband and now couldn't understand why the man was cheating on her.

"What I want is what I deserve," Bethany said, picking up her cup again and taking a tiny sip of tea. She reached into her bag again and came out with a bronze key. Lola was amazed at how quickly she found it, knowing that her own purse could swallow things whole and not regurgitate them for weeks.

"He told me it would be worth my while," Bethany continued as Lola took the key. It was nothing special and had 3 circles, a little like the Audi badge on one side and on the other was the number 256. She held it in her hand turning it over and over, and then pulled her attention back to the conversation.

"I need to know what the key is for. What has he hidden and where do I find it? Then I want to know what he is playing at. Is he back with his wife, is he cheating on her too? Is he coming back to me? There are so many questions I need answers to. Are you able to take the case?"

For a moment Lola was going to say no but there was something about the key that intrigued her. Why would a married man give a key to his mistress, his ex-wife, and then disappear? "I will take the case. I charge 500 pounds a day plus expenses." Lola had tripled her fees and she expected Bethany to turn her down but the woman simply nodded.

"How soon will you find something out?"

"I will start on the case tomorrow," Lola said. "I have other things I need to do first and I will let you know as soon as I find something."

Bethany nodded and stood. "I look forward to hearing from you," she said in a voice that contradicted the words.

Lola watched her walk out and let out a big sigh.

"Lady very angry," Sassy said in her mind.

"She certainly is," Lola agreed and was about to stand up.

"You sad," Sassy said. "Eat cake, feel better."

Lola laughed. "I think you might be right." Catching the eye of the waitress she ordered a slice of coffee fudge cake and while waiting for it to come she made a call to Alice, the woman who owned the property, and another to Sandra Johnson the wife of the man who had been found dead.

With two appointments made she sat back and enjoyed the cake. Just as the little Frenchie had said the delicious sweetness gave her a rush of endorphins which made her feel much better. The next stop was to have a look at the garage and see if she could find them a new home. After that, she would visit Sandra and decide if it was a case that she could take. There was a tinge of excitement for this was exactly the sort of case she wanted to investigate, but she knew she had to be careful. If this was simply Sandra's grief talking, it would be wrong to take her money for nothing. A touch of guilt flashed through her as she realized she was hoping it was foul play.

A NEW HOME

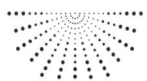

*L*ola pulled up outside the garage to see a pushbike waiting for them with a slim woman standing next to it. She was quite a sight dressed in a purple shell suit that looked like it had come straight from an 80's aerobics class topped by a smiling face and a short perm. She looked to be around 40 and Lola liked her instantly.

"You must be Lola, I'm Alice," she said holding out her hand for Lola to shake.

Lola took it, nodding her agreement, and was surprised at the firmness of the grip. "Thank you for meeting me."

"It's my pleasure," Alice squatted down and rubbed Sassy behind her ears. The little Frenchie grumbled and groaned with delight. "And you must be Sassy; Tilly told me so much about you too," Alice said standing up. "I don't need to ask how you found out about this place, Tilly is the best advertising money can't buy. Now, let me show you around."

"Best ear rub ever," Sassy said and Lola gave her a hurt expression.

"Well, best since this morning."

Lola smiled.

As Alice unlocked the door Lola wondered if she should bring Sassy in, but before she could ask, Alice was nodding.

"She's most welcome. Even if she wasn't a service dog, she would be most welcome in any of my houses. I used to have a Labrador." Her eyes clouded over for a moment. "I lost her last year, I'm not sure whether to get another one."

"I'm so sorry," Lola said already feeling close to this lovely woman. "You should, it would be great company."

"I know you're right, I wonder if Stuart will be having any puppies. He has a lovely black lab that is so sweet."

Lola nodded. "Is that the man on the big tractors?"

"It is, he's a real sweetie and single." Alice winked.

"Oh, no, I'm not looking… anyway, he's a little young for me."

"He smelt lovely of bull…"

"Sassy!" Lola didn't realize she had spoken out loud and Alice turned to see Sassy sniffing along the edges of the skirting in the reception area they had entered."

"She's ok," Alice said. "Come on in and don't worry, she can wander around wherever she likes."

The room they had walked into was large and airy surrounded by tall windows that looked out over the houses and across the surrounding countryside. It was an amazing view. Straight in front of them was a reception platform all in white and in front of the windows were dark brown seats that had seen better days. There was a residual smell of dust and engine oil. An oil stain marked the floor and Sassy was sniffing it.

"What this smell?" she asked.

"Engine oil," Lola said without thinking.

"Oh, sorry about that," Alice said. "The men who worked here were not the cleanest. I can have the place cleaned for you if you wish."

"Like the smell underground outside," Sassy said. "It covers something."

"Really, what?" Lola asked and then looked at Alice who had a raised eyebrow. "Sorry, I meant, no there's no need. I would have a full refurb done if I buy."

"I understand," Alice said. "The place could do with being stripped."

There were cupboards at the back and the whole area looked worn and a little scruffy. The floor was tiled a dull grey and three doors were leading off and a set of stairs disappeared out of sight.

"You're right it could do with a good refurb," Alice said. "Everything is a little dingy. You know what men are like when they are working on cars; they come in with greasy hands and put them everywhere."

Lola chuckled as she couldn't agree more.

"But I think the place has potential. Am I right that you run a small business?" Alice asked.

"I'm a Private Investigator," Lola said. "I'm living with my friend, Tanya, but I'm looking for a place of my own and this might be ideal. I could use the downstairs to interview my clients and maybe live above."

Alice clapped her hands in front of her and bounced up and down on her feet. "I'm so excited to have met a Private Investigator. You must lead such an interesting life. All I do is work at the library in Lincoln, read, and ride my bike in the countryside."

"That sounds like an idyllic life," Lola said as she wandered across to one of the doors. "May I?"

"Of course, take your time and look around. Would you like me to wait outside?"

Lola shook her head. "No, of course not, it's been lovely to talk to you." The first door Lola opened went into a small kitchen area. There was a table and four chairs in one corner. Two sides of the room had cupboards and a counter with the sink, next to that was a kettle. Once more the room was a little dingy and could do with a good clean but for a back-office room, it would need little else.

Sassy came in and had a good sniff around. "Was food, all gone now." Then she turned her little tail and ran back out of the room.

"She's a lively one," Alice said.

"She is that." Lola went back out and opened the next door; it was a restroom, with room for coats and a cupboard that looked like it had once held cleaning products and brooms. There were two cubicles and a sink all of which would need replacing.

The next door opened into what had once been an office. The floor was covered in what looked like mice droppings and the moment the door was open Sassy ran in. With her little tail held high, she ran backward and forwards across the room zigzagging and taking great big sniffs.

"So many smells. Little furry things. Me wants."

Lola chuckled.

"Oh, my, it looks like we've had a mouse. I will get that sorted and make sure that this is cleaned for you," Alice said, her hands fluttering in front of a face that had turned a nice crimson color.

"Don't worry about it," Lola said. "How long has the building been empty?"

Alice nodded her head a little bit as she thought. "It must be getting on for a year now. My brother, he's a lot older than me, he ended up in a home and I have to sell this place for him."

"I'm sorry to hear that," Lola said.

They walked into the next room which was similar to the one before but was lined with metal racking. Some of it had paper on them and there were a few car parts that she didn't recognize and the slight smell of oil. Cleaned out, it would be ideal as a storage room.

As they climbed the stairs Lola was starting to feel excited about her new place. Was she already thinking of it like that?

The stairs opened up into a large room with magnificent views over the countryside. It was obviously the living room and she could just imagine herself watching the sunset from that window.

The room was painted a dark brown that made it appear darker than it was. There was some furniture but all it really needed was a coat of paint and a few new pieces and it would be ideal.

"There's a small kitchen, one bedroom, and the bathroom is this way," Alice said as she turned to the left.

The kitchen was almost open plan with the living room. The two were separated by a breakfast bar made up of glass bricks of all different colors that reflected the light. Lola loved it instantly. The top was a dark grey marble in the kitchen, the units were dark grey shaker style and she loved them too. There was room for a washing machine, and fridge freezer and a sink was fitted.

Next to that was a small bedroom. It was really just a box room, and then the bathroom which was a horrible sage green.

The last room was a large bedroom painted all in white with dirty handprints on the wall. It had obviously been a man's room and needed a good clean and some more paint.

Lola loved it but she wondered what Sassy thought of it. As if she knew that Lola was thinking of her Sassy appeared in front of her. "What you think, girl? Lola asked.

"Me like, specially furry smell."

Lola chuckled and then realized that Alice was watching her. Instead of trying to explain she just shrugged and Alice smiled. Dog owners understood each other.

"I love it," Lola said and knew that she would be buying the place but right now she had to dash, for she had promised to meet Sandra Johnson to find out if there was a case there.

COULD IT BE MURDER

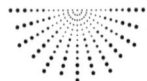

*L*ola stepped out of the car and walked up a long gravel drive towards an impressive-looking house. It was quite modern, three stories and at least six bedrooms. Though it didn't have the character of many houses in the village it was still very nice.

Either side of the drive was a neat but impressive garden. Rose bushes grew everywhere covered in flowers of every shade from pink through red to an almost dark purple. Behind the roses were lawns manicured to perfection. Someone was very proud of the garden.

With Sassy at her side, Lola approached the house and knocked gently on the oak door.

It was opened immediately by a tall and thin woman of around 35. Her hair was scraped back into a ponytail and her pale skin looked sallow against the black top she was wearing. Though obviously beautiful, she wore a heavy cloak of grief. Almost chocolate eyes were rimmed with red and squinting against the sunlight.

"I'm Lola Ramsey," Lola said holding out her hand. "First of all, let me give you my deepest condolences on the death of your husband."

Sandra took her hand and gave it a weak shake nodding to invite her in.

"This is Sassy, my service dog, are you all right if she comes in with me?"

"Of course. I'm Sandra Johnson and I really hope you can help me get some justice. I know my poor Fred didn't accidentally drown." Sandra took a crumpled and damp handkerchief from her pocket and wiped her eyes walking away as if she expected Lola to follow.

The house was all white, clean, and immaculate. They walked down the long hallway lined with photos of what looked like Sandra and Fred with two boys. The boys were very different but she didn't have time to look too closely before they ended up in a bright and ultra-modern kitchen.

It was a huge room with big picture windows looking out over a lawn surrounded by a seven or eight-foot-high leylandii hedge. The kitchen units were all white as was the floor and the ceiling and Lola had to blink, it all seemed so bright. She could see a drinks machine on the counter.

"Would you like me to make you a drink?" Lola asked.

"No, no, let me," Sandra said, walking to the side as if she was a zombie and waving her hand at the table.

Lola took a seat and waited.

Sandra put 2 cups of tea in front of them without asking how Lola took it. Though she normally took it black she took a sip and nodded her appreciation. "Why don't you tell me what you think happened," Lola said.

Sandra swallowed, her hands shaking as she tried to pick up the cup. Putting it back down, it rattled on the saucer before she turned moist eyes towards Lola. "Fred swam every day, sometimes two or three times a day; he loved that swim pond, it was his pride and joy."

Swim pond? Lola hadn't heard that expression and she wondered if it was a swimming pool and if Sandra was just tired.

"What did the police say?" Lola asked.

"They think he slipped, hit his head on a rock knocking himself out, and then drowned." Sandra took a sip of her tea and then her eyes widened as if she remembered something important.

Lola waited anxiously for she really didn't see a case here.

"I forgot, can I get you a biscuit?" Sandra asked, biting back her tears.

Lola reached out and took her hand ignoring the scratching on her leg.

"Cookie, me cookie," Sassy said in her mind.

"No, no, thank you," Lola said as she held the woman's hand offering what comfort she could. Sassy had been leaning against her leg and she felt the bulldog pull away. Though she may have a never-ending stomach she had also recognized the woman's stress and went up to offer her own form of comfort.

"Oh, my," Sandra said as she leaned back and scooped Sassy into her arms. Placing kisses on the back of the Frenchie's head, she took a few moments with her head bowed to control her emotions. "I'm so sorry. I keep telling myself I won't break down but it was all so sudden and so unfair."

Lola nodded her understanding and waited for Sandra to continue talking. She spoke about Fred and what a wonderful man he was. How he loved and cared for his family and how he would do anything for them. She spoke about the swim pond and how he had had it installed two years ago. "He used to say it just blends into the environment," Sandra said, "I loved it too but now… I just want to fill it in and never see it again."

"Why don't you show me where it happened?" Lola said. Though Sandra had told her many things, nothing had given her a reason to believe that this was anything other than a tragic accident.

Sandra nodded and they walked out of the kitchen, along the corridor and into a living room, and out of large French doors that opened onto another part of the garden. There in the middle of the grass was a beautiful pond but Lola would have described it as a lake. The water was crystal clear and reflected the beautiful blue of the sky. It was surrounded by pebbles of all shapes from small up to ones that must have been over a foot across.

There were a number of loungers on a concrete area on one side of the pond and two of them were occupied.

"They are my boys," Sandra said. "We should just say hello but I don't want to say too much in front of them."

"Of course," Lola said.

Sandra walked over and Lola followed with Sassy at her side.

"Evil bird," Sassy said, and pulling her lead from Lola's fingers she ran across the lawn to chase a crow that was close to the loungers. Missing the bird, Sassy circled back and went to the closest seat. There was a young boy of around 12 on it with his back to them. The way he was hunched over Lola imagined he was crying and she knew that Sassy would offer him comfort.

"Boys, this is Lola Ramsey, the lady I told you about," Sandra said forcing a smile onto her face. "She might want to ask you questions about your dad, you can tell her whatever you want."

The boy closest to them turned around; he was holding sassy and cuddling her close. He had soft brown hair and sunken chocolate eyes just like his mother's. They were lined with red and his face was sallow and smudged with dried tears.

"Do you want to say anything, Conner?" Sandra asked.

The young boy tried to look up but his face crumpled and with Sassy in his arms, he got up and raced across the grass into the house.

Sandra was about to follow him but Lola grabbed her arm gently. "Let him go. Just show me where it happened, there is no need for the children to go through this."

"But your dog?"

"Sassy is trained to help people deal with their emotions. Maybe she can help him."

Sandra nodded and then looked at the other boy. So far he hadn't lifted his head and was wearing headphones and no doubt pretending he couldn't hear.

"Tyler," Sandra said and there was a slight hint of nerves in her voice. Perhaps she was worried about upsetting him but before Lola could say anything the boy looked up.

There was something about him that Lola recognized but she couldn't place it. He had thick black hair styled into bed hair and dark eyes. A prominent chin supported a dimple and he was as pale as his brother. Lola got the feeling that if he smiled he would be a lovely-looking boy but there was something angry about him. There again, who wouldn't be angry if their father had just died.

"Do you have anything to say about your father?" Sandra asked.

Lola wanted to tell her to forget it, she didn't need to interrogate the boy for she was beginning to believe that this was just an accident.

Tyler simply shook his head and looked down again ignoring them.

"He's such a good boy," Sandra said and tried to smile.

"I know this is hard, why don't you show me what happened?" Lola said.

Sandra led her across the grass to where a wooden platform extended out over the water. It really was beautiful and idyllic and it looked like a real natural pond that you could come across out in the wilds.

"They are all the rage now," Sandra said. "Who wants a swimming pool when you can swim in nature?"

Lola agreed with her and studied the rocks and decking looking for clues.

She was just about to say that there was no case when her eyes noticed something and that familiar feeling of excitement ran down her spine. Could this really be a murder?

THE SWIM POND

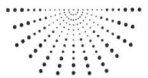

*L*ola wasn't sure why she felt the spark of excitement. As she looked around she couldn't see anything that looked out of place. The swim pond was idyllic and surrounded by the most perfect lawn she had ever seen. There was no sign of a scuffle, and nothing seemed out of place.

Letting her eyes drift over the water and around the edges of the pond she looked at the deck. Still, nothing explained why she felt so excited. The perfectly smooth rocks of all shapes and sizes made a stone beach leading into the pond all the way around. Not a stone was out of place, not a weed had been left and unpicked. Then she saw it.

Just to the right of the deck, the stones didn't look so

perfect. Walking over she studied them and sure enough, it looked to her that one had been removed and the others had been spaced back to make it difficult to tell. There was no mud, no footprints, nothing to make her believe that this was deliberate but somehow she did.

At that moment Sassy came running back to join her. "Boy sad but better now," Sassy said in Lola's mind.

"Can you sniff around here see what you can smell," Lola said and then looked around to see Sandra staring at her. "She's trained to sniff out certain things and indicate when she finds them." Lola shrugged her shoulders at Sandra and hoped the woman didn't think she was an apple short of a pie.

"Smell blood, people blood," Sassy said and sat down staring up at Lola with her big amber eyes.

"Clever girl," Lola said. Now she was convinced it was murder for if Fred had hit his head here then how had he drowned, for he was 5 feet away from the water? Yes, maybe he might have stood up and stumbled but that seemed a stretch a little too far.

"The police don't believe me," Sandra said, "but I know my husband and I know he didn't slip and drown. I don't care what it costs me, I want to know what really happened. Would you please take my case?"

Lola nodded. "I will charge you expenses and that is all. I do believe you but I'm not 100% sure that I can find you any proof or give you any closure. However, I will do my best."

Sandra took her hand and shook it warmly. "That is all I can ask, thank you, thank you so much. Do you need anything else?"

Lola asked for a few things, including a photo of Fred, and asked Sandra to keep her informed with anything the police told her. After giving Sandra her phone number, she returned to her car only to find Tyler leaning against it his headphones still on his head.

"Hey, Tyler, how you doing?" Lola asked.

"You need to leave us alone," he snapped. "What sort of ghoul tries to steal money off someone whose husband just died?"

Lola felt her heart begin to pound as her PTSD kicked in at his obvious antagonism. Taking a deep breath, she tried to stay calm. This was a sleepy English village, not Afghanistan there was no danger here.

A touch on her leg had her looking down and she saw Sassy smiling up at her. "All safe, all good, I bite him if he don't go away."

Lola felt a smile come on her face as her heart rate slowed.

"What you grinning at?" Tyler spat but this time it had no effect on Lola. "We don't want you here, take your mutt and get out." With that, he turned and stormed away.

Lola took a breath. "Thanks," she said and knelt down and rubbed Sassy behind her ears.

"Me like help," Sassy said. "Now me hungry." She was sat staring up at Lola with the most adorable look in her eyes that melted Lola's heart.

"We better go get you some foosty then," Lola said, using the word that meant Sassy's food.

Doing a little spin around Sassy barked and then sat in front of the car. "Hurry, hungry."

Lola laughed and unlocked the car climbing in and fastening the bulldog into her harness.

"Don't like him," Sassy said.

"I understand, but we all deal with grief in our own way."

"Don't like. All birds evil, bird me chase. Open door, now!"

"If I do then it will be longer before you get your food," Lola said hiding a chuckle as well as she could.

Sassy was looking out the window and her whole body shook with anticipation, but then the bird was gone. Poking out her bottom lip she sat down and turned to face Lola. "Bird escaped, hungry now."

Lola rubbed the little dog behind the ears and put the Jeep into drive.

WHO HATED FRED

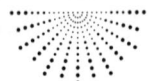

Lola made a few calls once Sassy had been fed. Firstly, she made an offer on the garage and it was accepted. Tanya had put her in touch with a solicitor and that was all arranged. Soon she would have a new home.

Over supper, she questioned Wayne about the case. He was the detective sergeant dealing with it and said that the police had written it off as an accident.

"I understand," Lola said, "but Mrs. Johnson has asked me to look into it. I have a feeling that there may be more to it."

For a moment Wayne froze and Lola felt a little intimidated. With dirty blond hair, hazel eyes, and a chiseled jaw, the man would not look out of place on the set of Baywatch — he did, however, seem out of place in this sleepy English village.

Those eyes were trained on her and he flexed his impressive shoulders under the t-shirt he had put on when he got home. Then he let out a sigh. "I felt the same way but there is no evidence to suggest foul play." For a moment he seemed to think about it and then a smile crossed his face. "I will tell you what I can... as you are representing the family I will do my best to help you."

"Great," Lola said.

"Still, hungry," Sassy said as she scratched Lola's leg under the table. She knew the Frenchie was getting fed enough but the dog seemed to have a bottomless stomach and she was always on the go so she must burn off a lot of energy.

"You're always hungry," Lola said passing her a little bit of gristle off her chicken. Then she blushed as Wayne and Tanya were staring at her.

"Sorry," Lola said, "the little monkey is scratching my leg begging for food. Now, back to the case."

As they continued eating, Wayne told her how they found the body, face down in the water, that there were no signs of a struggle and that the theory was he was unconscious when he hit the water and drowned. The police viewpoint was that he had slipped, hit his head, and fallen in. Case closed.

Lola still had that tingling feeling down her spine, the one she got when she was on to something interesting. What she had to decide, was if it was real, or if she was just feeling it because she didn't want to open the perfect peach folder and work on another cheating spouse.

* * *

Lola jolted awake, sweat-soaked, and panicked. She reached for her rifle but the calming thought in her mind brought her back to reality.

"Safe, home, loved," Sassy told her.

Lola felt her mind filled with love.

The little bulldog sat on the bed in front of her staring into her eyes and even if she couldn't hear and feel the love she could see it in those amber orbs.

Taking a big breath, Lola pushed images of Afghanistan out of her mind and focused on the day. Sunlight was streaming in around the dark blue curtains and she realized she had slept in, again. Even though she had been here several months, she still didn't seem to have kicked the jet lag.

Stretching, she got out of bed and went to the en-suite to take a shower. As she set the water running she peeked back into the bedroom. There was a morning ritual that she loved to see, it always put a smile on her face.

Lola had always had cold feet and much to the amusement of her once military colleagues she got into the habit of wearing socks in bed. Her current ones were fluffy and blue with purples spots on them. Of course, halfway through the night, her feet got too hot so she would take them off and tuck them behind her pillow.

Sassy sat on the bed looking as if butter wouldn't melt. Lola chuckled, butter wouldn't have time! As soon as Sassy thought she was gone the little bulldog stepped delicately over the pillow and sniffed behind it. Lola bit back a chuckle as Sassy appeared clutching the bed socks and then ran across the bed, jumped off and disappeared. For some reason, Sassy loved them, she loved all socks but these were her favorite. Though she never chewed them, she would carry them around for a few minutes before leaving them somewhere. Turning back to the shower, Lola was pleased it was her socks and not her knickers that the bulldog liked to steal.

The previous night Lola had written a letter to her friends, Melody and Alvin, back in Port Warren, USA. Melody was an excellent baker and owned a little shop. Along with her sheriff husband, she had become quite a little crimefighter and she had also helped Lola come to terms with her gift. Maybe one day Lola would go back and visit, or possibly even Melody and Alvin would come to the UK. With that thought in mind, she decided to post the letter and pick up some stamps from Tilly at the village shop. She also thought it would be a good idea to speak to Tilly about who could hate Fred enough to kill him.

Once dressed she glanced at the peach folder on her desk and decided it could wait for another time. The case about Fred was much more interesting.

As always Tilly was delighted to see her and invited them both into the back for a nice brew, as she called a cup of hot tea.

Lola sat down in the comfy chair in the room behind Tilly's shop while Tilly busied herself making the tea.

"Here, Sassy," Tilly called and offered the Frenchie a little bit of cake she had been eating. "Oh, I'm so sorry, is she all right having this?"

Lola chuckled. "I would be in trouble if I didn't allow her, don't worry it's fine."

Tilly popped the tea on the table and sat down. "How are you settling in?" she asked as she poured out 2 cups.

"Mine's black," Lola said, stopping Tilly from adding milk. "I'm doing really well and hopefully, I will have a new home soon."

"I've heard from Alice. Once things are sorted, if you need a builder I do happen to know a good one."

Lola chuckled, she should have known as much. She sipped her tea, it was really hot, she had forgotten to ask for a touch of cold water. "That would be really nice. I also wanted to say that I took Sandra Johnson's case. I'm not a hundred percent sure that it's murder but I do believe it warrants looking into." Taking a very cautious sip she wondered about the best way to approach Tilly about possible suspects. She shouldn't have worried.

"I've been thinking about that," Tilly said, jumping up and cutting two slices of a gorgeous-looking Victoria sponge cake. Passing one to Lola she sat down again. "I do hate to gossip, especially about the dead, but Fred wasn't well-liked. I could tell you a few people who had reason to want him... well, maybe not dead, but you know."

Lola nodded because she had just taken a bite of the sponge cake. It was light and delicious and the butter icing was so rich it just melted into the sponge. "That would be really useful," she said, once she had swallowed the cake. "Do you mind if I make a few notes?"

Tilly clapped her hands together and peered over her glasses, her little nose twitching just like a mole. "No, not at all. I am delighted to be involved in an investigation; it is so exciting."

Lola pulled out her notepad and waited.

"Well, as I said, Fred was not well-liked." Tilly leaned forward and whispered, "to be honest, I didn't like him much myself, a little arrogant and selfish if I do say so. Oh, isn't that awful of me?"

Lola shook her head. "No, you are an amazing person and I do believe sometimes we have to trust our instincts."

"You are very sweet, now where was I? Oh, yes, who would have a reason for killing Fred? Well, three people come to mind straightaway. The first one is Brent Burton. He was Fred's business partner and had been trying to buy Fred out for some time as far as I know. Now, Sandra won't admit this, but Fred was a bit of a womanizer. I believe this was causing problems with the business. Is that information helpful?"

"It most certainly is," Lola said. "Can you think of anyone else?"

Tilly nodded, her eyes bright and excited as she peered through her glasses. "There are two more people that I think would definitely have a bone to pick with him. The first one is Tony Munch. A lovely man, but he hates children and the Johnson children, well, Tyler can be a little too much. I know that the children teased him but that was not his main problem. I don't know whether you saw Fred's Leylandii hedge?"

"Yes, I did. I'm not a fan and it was quite a monster," Lola said shrugging her shoulders.

"Oh, you are right there, the whole village hates it. Now, those beautiful Yew hedges that line the road have been there for years. We all love them, but not that huge tall thing. If it was kept at a reasonable height it would be ok, but Tony's land backed onto Fred's garden. Since that hedge has grown it has stolen a lot of the light and much of the water from his garden. For a long while Tony was very good about it, but when nothing happened, and over the years the hedge just got taller and taller, so he lost his temper. I know they had fought over it in the past... though I had heard that now he was taking it through the courts."

"Interesting, neighborly disputes can often get nasty. Tempers flare and we all do things we don't intend to," Lola said, scribbling hastily in her book as Sassy tapped her leg and said, "cake," in her mind. Without thinking she broke off a small piece and slipped it to the Frenchie.

"Oh, no, I'm sure he wouldn't do anything awful... but I do think he had the motive to." Tilly sipped her own tea and took a delicate bite of the cake.

Lola nodded letting the details sink in and she thought of what to ask next. She was sure it couldn't be the children. Teasing could be very stressful, maybe that had added to Tony's anger. "You said the children teased Tony, do you know exactly what this involved?"

Tilly's cheeks flushed a little red and she nodded. "I hate to speak ill of people but the children were very mean. Tony, well, Tony's a little bit overweight and with his name being Tony Munch, the children were teasing him about how much he ate and they would call him Munch Munch. Tyler was the worst; don't quote me on this but I don't like that boy."

Lola made more notes and nodded. When children teased adults it could be so difficult. There was not a lot you could do to stop them if they wouldn't listen to reason and living next to that must've been very stressful. "You have given me two great suspects, thank you."

"Oh, my, I never intended them to be suspects..." Tilly's jaw had hit her chest and her eyes were wide. Then she chuckled a little bit. "I don't know whether to be excited or disgusted at myself for spreading this terrible gossip. However, I do have one other suspect, if that's what we're going to call them."

"Don't worry, Tilly, you aren't telling me anything that I won't investigate. I won't accuse people without verifying facts and without evidence. So don't worry about it one little bit."

"In that case, I will tell you about Clarissa Gee. You may have seen her riding around a bit on a big chestnut horse. She often rides with her friend on a bay, Naomi Owens, I think the friend is. They are two very nice girls but I do believe there are rumors." Tilly grinned a little bit but said no more and Lola decided not to push her.

"The village used to be so quiet, and all the traffic slow," Tilly said. "Fred had that big Jaguar and to my mind, he always drove a little too fast on these twisty narrow roads. I have heard that he had scared Clarissa's horse a time or two and when she confronted him about it, he called her a rather vicious name."

Lola looked up. "What did he call her?"

Tilly blushed scarlet this time. "It was a nasty word for being gay beginning with a D and ending in an E."

Lola scribbled it down and could understand how the woman would find this offensive. If she loved the horses, which Lola was sure she did, and Fred was making it hard for her to ride then that must have made things pretty unbearable. If a horse was to bolt on the narrow roads, with the yew hedges almost up to the road, there would be nowhere for the horse to go but into the traffic. Tilly was right; the streets were quiet but one fast car was all it took for disaster. This was something that she would definitely look into. Maybe Fred pushed Clarissa past her limits. "That is great information," Lola said.

"Well, I can probably think of a few more people but these are the ones that come to mind first," Tilly said.

Lola skipped her eyes over the notes. It certainly looked like Fred had a number of enemies. Now she just had to work out if one of them was a killer.

LET'S INVESTIGATE

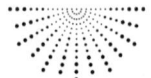

*L*ola quickly looked up the phone number of the architect firm that Brent Burton now controlled. It had a slick website with a black band across the bottom of the home page and the page for Fred Johnson. The picture of Fred was much better than the one that Sandra had shown her. He was a slick-looking man that knew he was attractive. Soft brown hair reminded her of Tyler but the eyes were very different, knowing, predatory. The suit he wore was blue a touch lighter than navy and it was a color to impress, to show off his prowess. Lola clicked onto the page for Brent Burton.

The man was also attractive and had a presence that came through the screen. Short black hair was peppered with grey that gave him a distinguished look. His eyes were a piercing grey and there was something a little sharkish about his smile. Wearing a very smart dark grey suit he looked every bit the professional businessman. Comparing him to Fred showed the difference. Though on his own, Fred looked business-like, next to Brent he was coarser. For a moment, Lola thought of a gigolo in an old film she had seen. It was not the perfect description but it was the difference between them. Fred was all about the image and the image was to attract the opposite sex. Brent was also, all about the image, but his was power and professionalism.

Lola called the company's reception and asked to make an appointment. At first, she thought they were going to put her off but when she pleaded that Sandra Johnson had asked if she could speak to Brent she was put on hold. Classical music kept her waiting for just a minute and she was invited in to see Brent in an hour. It was perfect, she had time to grab a coffee and get to the address shown. It was in an industrial estate at the top of Lincoln and would only take her ten minutes to drive there.

Lola pulled up in the parking lot, or car park, and checked her reflection in the vanity mirror. She quickly added a touch of lipstick and ran a hand over her hair. Today was one of its flyaway days and it kept wanting to stick up all over. Once it was tamed a little she clipped a lead onto Sassy's harness and opened the door.

The Frenchie waited while Lola checked it was safe and then jumped out when told. Lola followed and made her way across the tarmac to the ultra-modern building. It was large and three-story. Burton and Johnson were doing all right for themselves. Near to the door was a large silver-gray Mercedes with the registration number BR11 ENT.

"Looks like he's in," Lola said.

"Steak," Sassy said in return.

Lola sniffed the air and looked around. There was a steak house just across the road, it was obvious that the Frenchie was more interested in that than the offices. Lola couldn't blame her but this was where the investigation had led them.

"Tonight," she said, "for now tell me all about the people inside."

Sassy looked mournfully at the source of the delicious smells and then wagging her tail turned and headed towards the door.

The receptionist was an attractive middle-aged woman who was smart and efficient. When they entered her eyebrows rose but she spotted Sassy's yellow service jacket and relaxed.

"I'm here to see Mr. Burton; I'm Lola Ramsay and we spoke on the phone," Lola said.

"Of course, please sign in and I will have you shown up." She buzzed a number and spoke into the phone and almost before Lola had finished signing, the elevator doors behind her opened and a smart, middle-aged woman with a blonde bob and a pinstriped skirt suit stepped out.

"I'm Mrs. Morgan, please follow me," she said and turned back to the elevator.

The elevator was glass, modern and spotless. Lola and Sassy followed her in.

As the doors closed Sassy poked out her bottom lip and hunkered down a little. Lola wanted to ask her what was wrong but Mrs. Morgan interrupted her.

"We were all very sorry to hear about Mr. Johnson," she said. "I hope you will pass our condolences on for us."

The elevator moved upwards

"Tummy come back," Sassy shrieked.

Lola bit her tongue as she was just about to answer and had to bite back the chuckle that would have been most inappropriate. Instead, she moved her leg closer to touch Sassy as the Frenchie often did for her.

"Of course, she is devastated as you must all be. I guess she just wants answers."

Mrs. Morgan nodded but said no more and then they were there and the doors opened onto a wide landing in cream with gold coving. It was lush and expensively appointed as well as being very stylish. Mrs. Morgan stepped to the right where there was a desk and office area in front of large glass windows opening into what could only be Brent's office.

Lola glanced in the opposite direction and saw a mirror image, no doubt Fred's office. At the PA's desk, a woman sat with her blonde head bowed. Was that Fred's PA? Was he having an affair with her and would she have a motive? These questions all nagged at Lola as she was shown to Fred's office.

A TOUCH OF JEALOUSY

*L*ola looked across as Brent rose from his desk and walked towards her. The shark smile was even more prominent in the sad expression on his face. It didn't seem genuine and his dead grey eyes seemed to see right through her. She had decided to tell Brent that Sandra was convinced that Fred had been murdered and that she suspected everyone. Lola would make out she didn't believe her but was going through the motions. Looking at this man now, she knew it was the right play.

"Mr. Burton, I'm sorry for your loss," she said as they shook hands.

Brent nodded looking suitably sad, his grip was tight, too tight but he didn't count on the fact that Lola was a veteran and had needed to stand her ground with the toughest. She returned the pressure just as hard and was pleased to see him wince a little.

Returning to his desk he offered refreshments.

"No, that's fine," Lola said. "I won't keep you long." Quickly she explained.

"I am so sorry, we are all so shocked about Fred, and Sandra must be too. I can understand her feelings, we never want to believe these things and hopefully, you can put her mind at ease."

"I hope so," Lola said.

"Man not really sad," Sassy said as she sniffed the air at Lola's side. Her little snub nose was raised and her bottom lip was once more out with that petulant little look. "He's happy, joyous, and relieved."

Lola was amazed that the dog could tell that from just a quick sniff but she had seen dogs that knew when a friend's blood sugar was dropping before the blood monitor could pick it up. It totally amazed her what dogs could discern. Right now, she trusted Sassy's judgment for she got a bad feeling about this guy; he was hiding something. Now all she had to do was find out what.

"Is there anything I can do to help?" Brent asked.

Lola dipped her chin to adopt a look of embarrassment. "I really hate to do this but Sandra wonders if you may have a motive to kill Fred, Mr. Johnson. I know it's ridiculous but do you have an alibi?"

Brent laughed, a loud explosive sound as he sat more upright, squared his shoulders making himself bigger and more masculine. It was a gesture Lola had been taught to recognize in the military. Men would lean back, open their arms and sometimes legs to subconsciously adopt a more threatening stance. Some didn't know they were doing it but she got the feeling that Brent did.

"An alibi, well, luckily for me, dear, I was in London." The tone of voice was condescending now. "Really, Sandra is such a silly billy." The look on his face was no longer sad but overbearing and arrogant; then, as if catching himself, he let his smile droop and rubbed a hand across his brow. "Losing Fred is a major blow to the business, forgetting my personal loss. He was half of this company and going forward will mean some big changes that will be challenging. Do you have any more questions? I do have a very busy day."

"No, I think I have all I need, for now. I'm sure this is all a mix-up and I can put Sandra's mind at ease. Thank you for your time and you have a good day now."

As if she had been listening in, the door opened and Mrs. Morgan came to escort her out. Lola noticed the expression she had as she looked across at the matching desk to hers. The woman who sat there, still had her head bowed.

Intrigued, Lola dropped her bag and the contents spilled onto the floor. Sassy sniffed around at them and then feeling the lead drop she trotted across to the other woman.

"I'm so sorry," Lola said. "I'm so clumsy today."

Mrs. Morgan's face relaxed. "We all get days like it."

Bending down and slowly gathering her things, Lola searched her mind for what to say. What did she want to gain from this woman? Well, her reaction to Fred's PA was certainly interesting.

"I'm so sorry about Mr. Johnson," Lola said. "Is that his assistant?" she used the lesser word hoping it would help.

"Yes, she was Fred's secretary. Hopefully, the floozy will be gone soon. No one else would want her."

Lola felt a touch of excitement, she had hit on something. "Can you fill me in a little on Fred? I'm working for Sandra and I get the feeling she has her own viewpoint of the man. What was yours and how did he fit in here?"

For a moment her face closed down and then she nodded and smiled. "You will find out anyway so I may as well tell you. Fred was a nightmare. He couldn't keep his hands and eyes off the ladies."

Ladies was said as if it left a bad taste on her tongue and once more her eyes flicked across the room. It looked like there was some rivalry there.

"Was there any trouble?" Lola asked, pleased to see that Sassy had found a new friend in the woman across the landing.

"Oh, there was certainly trouble. A string of affairs." Once more her eyes moved pointedly to her rival. "I believe he had just finished one, who knows what can happen in such circumstances. Then there was trouble with HR, complaints, discipline that came to nothing, and one or two payments had to be made... to keep the *ladies* quiet. I wouldn't be surprised if his wife got sick of him... I know I would have."

Lola could see her close down, Mrs. Morgan was realizing that she had said too much.

Lola thanked her. This visit had certainly given her a lot to think about.

"Would you like me to see you down?" Mrs. Morgan asked.

"No, I'm good. I'll just get Sassy and I might as well question your friend." Lola winked and got a little smile in return.

"I am sorry he's dead," Mrs. Morgan said, "but not that he's gone. Mr. Burton will finally be able to relax and build for the future."

Lola nodded and walked across the intervening space. That had certainly been illuminating. Brent had an alibi but he also had a motive. Reading between the lines, a lot of motive and he had money. Could he have hired a hitman?

It looked like she still had a suspect in Brent. And what about the woman who was cuddling Sassy? It was obvious that Mrs. Morgan thought she had had an affair with the boss. If it ended badly... such things had a habit of going wrong. Maybe this was another suspect?

A BIG RELIEF

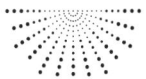

"Hi, I'm Lola." Lola arrived at the woman's desk, she was still leaning over Sassy, all she could see was a long mane of blonde hair.

"Sad lady, nice lady," Sassy said, her eyes all dreamy as she enjoyed the scratch she was getting.

"Sorry." The woman sat up and she was a knockout. Perfect features, big dreamy blue eyes, and a figure that men would weep over. Though her clothing was meant to draw the eye, Lola noticed that her three-inch heels were kicked off under her desk. There was something incongruent about the two looks.

The beautiful eyes were red-rimmed, and her sadness was genuine. Wiping at her face she leaned back. "Do you want your dog back? She is lovely."

"Are you okay?" Lola asked.

"I guess... I'm Louisa," she said, "Louisa Meek and... well it is just so hard to understand."

"I'm pleased to meet you, Louisa, I'm Lola Ramsay. Why don't we go get a coffee? I'm sure you could use a break."

Louisa's smile was one of relief as if she had been saved. "Would you mind going down and I will meet you in just a moment? I don't want the dragon lady to know or she will make comments."

Lola nodded and picking up Sassy's lead she turned to leave, giving a conspiratorial nod in the direction of the other desk. Best to keep the dragon lady thinking she was on her side.

* * *

Some minutes later and Lola, Louisa, and Sassy were sat outside drinking cappuccinos and eating cake. The cafe was on the edge of a lake and very busy. Sassy was sitting under the table leaning against Lola's leg for two tables away was a very angry Chihuahua that didn't seem to want her there. The little terror was barking and raging while sat on a woman's knee. The woman appeared to not even notice. Lola reached down and rubbed Sassy between the ears, the little Frenchie grunted her appreciation.

"How are you doing?" Lola asked bringing her attention back to Louisa.

Louisa let out a big sigh. "It's been such a shock. Mr. Johnson was my boss, I've worked for him for six months and this is my first real job... I guess... well, I guess I just never expected something like this and my emotions are all over the place."

"Were you close?" Lola asked.

Color flushed up Louisa's cheeks and she bowed her head. "I guess."

Lola knew the girl was hiding something and she suspected it was the affair and that her grief was genuine; however, it wasn't the raw grief of someone who had lost a lover. Something was going on here. "As I'm sure you're aware Mrs. Morgan told me you were having an affair with Fred. That must make this incredibly hard for you."

"I guess," Louisa said before taking a sip of her drink and letting her hair fall down like a shield between them.

"I really want to be your friend," Lola said and she felt Sassy leave her side going around the chair but keeping under the table and out of the way of the chihuahua before venturing to sit in front of Louisa.

Louisa pulled back and picked up the little Frenchie, cuddling her close.

Lola decided she had to ask the question and thought it was best to get it out of the way now. "I'm sorry to ask you this but do you have an alibi for when Fred was murdered?"

Louisa looked up from Sassy her eyes wide, her mouth open. "I thought it was an accident."

"Oops," Sassy said in Lola's mind.

"Well, yes, you are right, the police have put it down as an accident. Sandra, Mr. Johnson's wife, is not so sure… and I tend to agree with her. There are unanswered questions and I hate to ask you, but where were you on Saturday around 3 PM?"

"It's okay, and I'm bound to be a suspect. I don't have an alibi as such I guess, I was painting. I was set up near the cathedral so maybe someone saw me. I did stop at the stand there for a coffee a couple of times, but I can't say to you so-and-so saw me."

"That's okay, I'm sure you can prove that. If I need to get evidence, there is bound to be CCTV up there. I'd love to see your painting sometime. My friend, Tanya, is an amazing artist, but I'm pretty useless. I even fail at drawing a stick man."

Louisa chuckled and pulled out her phone scrolling through and passing it over.

Lola was impressed, it wasn't finished but it was amazing and the pieces that were finished were almost as good as a photograph. "Wow, you have a real talent, you should do this for a living."

Louisa dropped her head again and her shoulders seemed to slump. "I wish I could afford to, I hate working at the office... I hated everything about it but I need the money. My mum lost her job last year and we're only just meeting the bills."

"I'm so sorry to hear that, maybe you could build your painting up on the side?"

"It doesn't really matter now, without Mr. Johnson I won't have a job."

Lola noticed as she said Mr. Johnson she closed down. She was definitely hiding something about him Lola just didn't know what. Her instinct told her that it was something bad, something traumatic. Which, of course, could be that she had murdered him. However, Lola's gut told her that it was something else. "You can confide in me."

Louisa shrugged as if she didn't understand what Lola was saying.

"You see that Sassy's wearing a service jacket."

Louisa nodded. "I did wonder why... but didn't want to ask."

"I was in the military. I saw a lot of horrible things. When I got back, silly things like doors slamming, any banging, any shouting or conflict... well, it was bad for me. I only started to get better when I talked to people about it. Now Sassy helps. She senses my stress and is there to ground me. Now, she senses your stress, whatever it is, you can talk to me."

The two sat and drank and munched on the cake for another 15 minutes. Slowly, gently Lola probed Louise about her time in the job. Then it dawned on her and she wondered if maybe Fred Johnson got what he deserved.

"How did you get the job?"

Louisa let out a sigh. "Fred saw me painting one day and bought me a drink. This carried on for a while and at first, there was no pressure. I was in awe of this handsome man paying me so much attention. He always had money and treated me to so much and he was complimentary, if cheeky. Then, when my mum lost her job, he started to say he knew a way I could earn some money. At first, I was horrified. I thought he was asking me to become a prostitute. He backed down quickly and said he was looking for a secretary but... well, it was implied that if I wanted the job that I would date him. I don't know how it really happened; he bought me clothes I don't like." Her hands flashed up in the air and down her body. "You wouldn't catch me dead wearing these before Fred."

Lola swallowed but was determined to stay calm to help this poor woman through the ordeal. "Did he force you?"

Louisa shook her head vehemently. "No, it was never force... it was just... pressure." Dropping her head she began to cry and all Lola could do was reach out and hold her hand as she hugged the little bulldog and let her hurt come out. "I'd been trying to break it off for a while, but couldn't."

Lola sat quietly and waited for Louisa to finish. When she did, she handed her a clean handkerchief.

Louisa looked up and it was as if the world had been lifted from her shoulders. Her face was bright or more alert and her eyes shone with optimism. "I'm sorry if I was foolish. I guess I'm not the only young girl to be fooled by an older married man."

"No, you're not, but that doesn't make it right. What are you going to do now?"

"As daft as it seems I feel better already. I applied for a job at one of the local restaurants and got it. It won't be enough, but it's better than nothing. If only I could sell one of my paintings or two then I could make things work."

"I'm sure you will do. In fact, I will buy the picture of the cathedral for my new office and I would like to commission you to do a picture of Sassy for me. There, you have your first commissions and I'm sure more will come in soon."

"Oh, safe at last," Sassy said in Lola's mind.

Lola looked up to see the woman with the little mean dog walking away.

"Can I take your phone number?" Lola asked.

"Of course, if there is anything I can do to help let me know," Louisa said with a sweet smile.

Lola got up but before she walked away she decided to ask one more question. Pulling out the key she showed it to Louisa. "Do you have any idea what this is for?"

Louisa took it and turned it over. "I might, Mr. Johnson got me to do a lot of things for him and this rings a bell." Taking out her phone she snapped a picture of the key. "Leave it with me and I will check the records at the office. I'm not sure how long I will be welcome there for, but I will do my best."

"Thank you."

A SECRET REVEALED

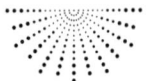

Lola's next stop was back at the village, she intended to look through the file that Bethany Price-Williams had given her. So far, she had got nowhere on her case with Mr. Johnson. She had all but eliminated one suspect as she did not believe that Louisa was the killer. Brent, however, still could be. It was only as she drove back that she realized she still hadn't looked at the apricot file and she felt a little guilty for being so unprofessional.

Turning down the hill into the quiet village of South-Brooke she was once again struck by its beauty. The fabulous yew hedges it was renowned for looked so perfect they could almost be a picture. Hanging over them were roses of all shapes and colors and she took a moment to just take in the beauty of it. That was when she saw a woman leading a horse further down the road. It had to be Clarissa Gee, another one of her suspects. This seemed like an opportunity too good to miss, so she drove down slowly and followed the horse into the stable yard it had turned into.

It was a very impressive property; a big house to the left and a block of what looked like 10 stables to the right. They were beautifully maintained and horses' heads were showing over three of them. Behind the stables, she could see paddocks and a menage lined with mirrors. It looked like Clarissa was committed to her sport.

Lola parked her Jeep to one side and was about to get out when there was a knock on her window. A vision of carnage flashed through her mind; her hands tightened on the wheel gripping it until her knuckles were white.

"Safe, love, safe," Sassy said in her mind and moved over to lick her arm.

Letting out a breath Lola nodded her head, she was back here in the present and had escaped the vision that came to her. Turning, she saw a woman in her mid-30s with a handsome face and wearing a riding hat peering in the window.

"I'm so sorry, I didn't mean to surprise you," the woman said. "I just wondered if I could help."

Lola shook her head and got out of the car holding out her hand. "No, it's... it's my fault. My name is Lola Ramsey and I'm sorry to bother you but I'm working for Sandra Johnson." Before her stood a handsome woman immaculately dressed and presented in a cream blouse and cream jodhpurs, with a black jacket and matching black hat. There was a cream cravat at her throat with a gold pin holding it in place. It was all very neat and very British. Considering she had just walked the horse into the yard Lola was amazed that the jodhpurs and blouse were so clean and bright and the long black riding boots she wore were polished almost to perfection. She had on a hint of lipstick and nothing else and her smile was guarded but friendly.

"Oh, please accept my condolences for Fred's death. I'm Clarissa, Clarissa Gee. We didn't get on too well, Fred and I, but I really am sorry to hear of his passing."

"It's a tragedy," Lola said, "and please forgive me, but Mrs. Johnson believes there may have been foul play and she has tasked me to just ask around and do a little bit of investigating."

"Horsey droppings, the best to roll in," Sassy said.

Lola bit back a chuckle and sent back an image of a bath with Sassy in it. It was something she was trying and this was the first real experiment.

Sassy let out a big grunt of disgust. "Hate baths."

It looked like it worked.

Clarissa removed her riding hat and her long auburn hair streamed down around her shoulders. With brown eyes and a nose a little too large she was still a handsome woman but it was obvious she had spent a lot of time in the sun and her cheeks were deeply tanned, her eyes lined with crow's feet. Lola was expecting her to resist, to protest her innocence, and ask for her to leave but instead, she smiled.

"I understand completely. You may have heard that Fred had a tendency to drive too fast down the narrow lanes. On more than one occasion he had scared my horses. It could have caused an accident and that made me incredibly angry. I would never, however, do anyone any harm. I don't even eat meat."

"I'm so sorry to hear about that; why would anyone drive fast around here?"

Clarissa flushed, her bronze cheeks pinking. "I believe it was because he doesn't like people like me," she said. "Oh, just in case you need to know, I do have an alibi."

Both the blushing and the offer of an alibi surprised Lola. Why would an innocent person have an alibi? There again, who didn't watch TV programs of cops and criminals nowadays? If anyone was questioning you, I guess it was pretty obvious they were looking for an alibi. "Of course, I'm sure you do," Lola said but there was something about the way that Clarissa had blushed that made her wonder. So far, the woman had been open and direct and this was no blushing youngster like Louisa, this was a mature and successful woman, so what was she hiding?

"Yes, I was riding with my friend, Naomi Owens. I can give you her number if you wish or I can arrange for a meeting for you to talk to her."

"Lady lying but not bad," Sassy said in Lola's mind.

"What time exactly was that?" Lola asked.

Clarissa blushed even more and looked down coughing. "Oh, well, I was... I was there Friday night... sometimes I stay, she is my friend and we went riding the next morning."

"Thank you for that," Lola said. She now understood why Clarissa was worried. Naomi was probably more than just a friend and in a small village like this, gossip could be cruel. It made perfect sense why Fred would be mean to her as she was starting to get a not very nice picture of the man. "Well, I won't take up any more of your time. If I need anything, am I okay to call and see you?"

"Yes, of course, and if you ever fancy going for a ride, I have some quiet horses that I'm sure you would love."

"Thank you so very much. I just moved here and I'm finding this village so friendly."

"Most of us are," Clarissa said before turning and walking away.

Lola drove back quickly to find the house empty. Tanya must be taking a class and Wayne would be at work.

Making herself a quick coffee and feeding Sassy she retired to her room. There on the desk was the apricot folder. Placing her coffee on the desk next to it she pulled out the chair and sat down. Maybe it wasn't as exciting as a murder but, Bethany deserved an answer.

Taking a sip of coffee she opened the file and almost dropped her cup.

A WOMAN SCORNED

*L*ola was stunned, the picture staring back at her from the apricot file was none other than Fred Johnson. What was going on here and was his murder to do with the key?

Lola quickly read through the file but it gave her nothing but his name, age, date of birth, dates of marriage. Bethany then listed what she considered were his affairs and there were photos to prove some of them. Then there was a list of what she got out of the marriage when they divorced and another list of what she wanted. Top of that list was the house that Sandra Johnson now lived in.

Lola's mind was turning over and over, did Bethany have a motive to kill him? Well, her bitterness about the affairs would definitely be a motive but looking at this file she would gain nothing once he was dead. The house and income, any insurance would go to his current wife and the key was still a mystery.

So, logically, she had no motive to kill him but a woman scorned is rarely logical. There was every possibility that she could have lost her temper.

***

The following morning Lola showered and dressed trying to work out if she had missed anything. She still had Tony Munch to visit so hopefully, she had another suspect.

Pulling the comb through her hair she turned around to see Sassy sitting in front of her with her bed socks in her mouth.

"Mine, tasty," Sassy said before turning on a dime and running out of the room.

Chuckling to herself, Lola followed her down the stairs to find her in the kitchen. Tanya was making toast and Wayne was sat at the table drinking tea and reading the paper. Sassy sat in front of Tanya, perched on her hind legs, her front paws waving in the air begging for food, but she refused to let go of the socks.

"Morning, Lola," Tanya said, "this dog of yours is crazy."

"Don't I know it." Lola took a piece of crust off the surface and sat at the table opposite Wayne. "Swapsies," she called.

"Not fair!" Sassy said in her mind but she trotted over and handed over the socks in return for a piece of the toast.

Lola tucked them in her back pocket and poured herself a black tea.

"Do you want some toast?" Tanya asked as she buttered another two rounds and piled them on a plate. The plate was then passed over to the table along with a jar of marmalade and a jar of raspberry jelly, or jam as it was called in England.

"Oh, yes please, but I can make it," Lola said.

"No need, I've probably done way more than we need." Tanya put two more rounds on a plate and carried it to the table sitting down next to Lola.

Lola quickly gave Sassy her breakfast and then joined them at the table.

For a few minutes, there was nothing but the sound of scraping jam onto the toast and munching and sipping as they all enjoyed the breakfast. Sassy had wolfed down her kibble as quickly as if it wasn't there. She was now sitting next to the table and would occasionally tap Lola's leg or tell her that she was hungry.

Lola was dying to tell her that she couldn't still be hungry but of course, she couldn't. Once the breakfast was finished they began to talk again.

"How's the case going?" Wayne asked.

Lola ran through her suspects starting with Clarissa and ending with Louisa. Wayne gave his input and they both agreed that Brent was probably the best bet out of the three.

"I wanted to discuss Louisa with you," Lola said.

"I understand, but I don't think she's a suspect," Wayne said.

"Oh, no, I'm sorry, I meant with Tanya."

"I don't see how I can help," Tanya said.

That was when Lola told her about her wish to be a painter and how she had kind of bought two of them. "She's really talented and she's struggling so much I just wonder what I can do to help her. She was taken advantage of and she deserves a better life."

Wayne held up his hand. "Whoa, let me stop you right there. She is not your responsibility and you can't think like this. Trust me, if you do you will exhaust yourself both mentally and physically very quickly. You can prove her guilt or innocence but you can't take responsibility for her life, it's not up to you it's up to her."

"I only wanted to help," Lola said.

"Hold on a moment," Tanya said interrupting the conversation. "As an outsider to this discussion, I see what both of you mean. Lola, Wayne is right, you cannot take the whole of the world's problems on your shoulders. Wayne, Lola was right, if you can help somebody then why wouldn't you? I tell you what I'll do, let me see one of her paintings and maybe I can pull some strings. Don't say anything yet, as I'm not promising anything."

"You are just the best," Lola said jumping up and putting her arms around Tanya. "And I mean both of you," she said smiling at Wayne.

After breakfast Lola decided to go and see Tony Munch, she also knew she had to go see Bethany again but she wanted to find out more about the key. Unfortunately, Wayne wasn't able to give her much help with that, but he had said he would look into it.

Tony's place backed onto Fred Johnson's garden. They were both in the village and so Lola decided to walk. With a notebook and phone in her bag and Sassy on her harness they were about to set off. As they got to the door she could swear that she could feel Sassy laughing.

"Okay, what is it?"

"You have my socks," Sassy said.

Lola patted her back pocket to find the socks still in there. With a chuckle, she walked upstairs and left them in the bedroom. "Okay, little miss sock thief, any other fashion tips?"

"Need a tiara."

"Me or you?"

"Me, Princess Sassy."

Lola quickly checked her phone for the order that was due in a few days, it still said it was on the way. "Well, if you're a really good dog and help solve this case, who knows."

Sassy spun in a circle and did a quick bark before sitting and staring up at the door. "Me good. Nose on overdrive."

"Great, you tell me what you think about the people we meet and we will solve this in no time."

"Then I get my tiara?"

"We'll see."

It was just a 10-minute walk to Tony's property. As they stepped onto the drive Lola could see his garden at the back of the house and could fully understand why he had a problem. This was one of the village's smaller gardens, but it was still a substantial size and looked well loved and cared for though not quite as manicured as Fred's. However, the huge Leylandii hedge that towered over it blocked out most of the sun and must've been a massive job to keep trimmed.

The house itself was a nice two-story house with two windows on either side of the door on both levels. A rose arch with a beautiful deep damask rose framed the front door that was painted a dark green. Lola lifted her hand to knock and the door was opened by a thick-set man who had a big smile on his face. He was a little overweight with brown hair cut into an old-fashioned neat and tidy haircut. There was something sweet about him and Lola knew she shouldn't think this way but she couldn't believe he was a killer.

Reaching out her hand she said, "good morning, I'm Lola Ramsey and I'm working for Sandra Johnson. I wonder if you'd mind if I ask you a few questions?"

Tony's smile faltered but then he looked down and noticed Sassy at Lola's feet. Once again a huge smile was plastered all over his face and he nodded. "Good morning, come on in and I'll put some tea on."

He led Lola through a well-ordered house that was a little bit old-fashioned in its furniture and out into a conservatory. The room looked out over the gardens and was shaded by the hedge.

Lola sat down on a wicker chair and waited. Very soon he came through with a tray and sat on a matching chair opposite her.

"What's her name?" Tony asked as he poured the tea.

"She's called Sassy, no milk or sugar please."

Tony laughed and handed over the tea. "It suits her, may I?"

Lola unclipped the lead and let Sassy go to him. She was pulled up onto his lap and was soon in heaven as he rubbed behind her ears. For a few moments, he was happy with the dog and Lola took a sip of the tea. It was strong and good and she couldn't believe how much she was enjoying tea since she'd been in England.

"Well, I guess I know what you want to talk to me about," Tony said.

"I'm sorry, I have to ask some questions that's all," Lola said.

"Not a problem. And I'll admit now, I'm not sad that he's gone. Fred was not a nice man and he made my life hell. There again, I'm not the only one he did that to. However, I would never have killed him. I wanted my satisfaction in the courts. I wanted to see his face when I got a bulldozer in to rip that… blooming hedge out."

Lola could see his passion but once more she didn't see a killer, just a frustrated man who wanted justice. In many ways, Fred's death had denied him that. Yet it was conceivable that he lost his temper and struck out. That an argument had turned bad. "I totally understand, but I also have to ask if you have an alibi?"

"Luckily, I do. I was helping out at the church which I quite often do in my spare time. I have to say, that boy of his, Tyler, he's not a nice child. A lot of people want him gone from the village."

Lola remembered Tilly telling her that Tyler and his friends teased Tony. "What sort of things did Tyler get up to?" She wasn't sure why she was asking this because it didn't really relate to the case but, sometimes you had to follow where the lead led.

"You name it, loud music, swearing, the wacky backy, he's mean to dogs and chases them. He teased me as well as lots of other people. The boy is just bad to the bone."

"Thank you for being so honest with me, you've been a real big help."

Tony gave Sassy another big hug and then put her back down on the floor. "Me, I love dogs, I lost my spaniel last year and I haven't been able to get another one yet. Too many memories. You can bring this little sweetie to see me anytime you want."

Lola said her goodbyes and decided to walk up to the church and see if she could corroborate Tony's alibi. However, she didn't really think she needed to, her gut told her he wasn't guilty.

BACK ON THE SUSPECT LIST

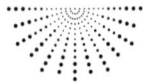

Sassy and Lola made the five-minute walk up to the local church. It was a beautiful building, with the most wonderful stained-glass windows that sent sparkles of color across the grass. Tall trees shaded the cemetery and gave the place the allusion of an oasis of tranquility in a busy world. There was something peaceful about it and on other occasions, they had wandered around looking at the old gravestones and just soaking in the history. However, today she was here to work and she wanted to find the vicar. She had been to a few services and found the man very likable. There was no fire and brimstone in Father Jackson's preaching. On the contrary, he believed that God was a caring God that loved all of us.

Lola knew that his house was behind the church. After taking a quick look around, she couldn't see him so she headed around the back.

"Can I help you, child?" Father Jackson stood up from behind a hedge and almost frightened Lola out of her skin.

Her heart was pounding, sweat appeared on her forehead, and she clenched her fists to fight back the visions that wanted to flood her mind.

Sassy touched her leg with her nose and sent feelings of love and warmth. "Safe, funny man hiding."

Lola swallowed. "Good morning, Father," she managed in a croak, "I'm sorry to disturb you if you were busy in your garden. I just wondered if I could ask you a few questions?"

The father dusted down his hands and led her across the garden to a table under a beautiful yellow rose that draped across a pergola and scented the air with peach. "I'm sorry if I startled you," he said. "Can I get you some tea?"

Lola was already having to fight back the giggles at the thought of the father hiding behind the hedge to jump out at her that her bulldog had put in her mind. Now, she felt as if the world and this village revolved around drinking tea. Though she was sure the feeling was slightly to do with the shock, the startle that her body had just been through, she had a terrible urge to giggle and had to bite it down.

"Bless you Father, but I've had tea at Tony Munch's not 10 minutes ago and I don't think I'd better have anymore."

"Of course, of course, Tony is a wonderful man and so helpful to me. Now, how can I help you?"

Before she could answer, Lola felt Sassy straining on her lead. In the corner of the garden, a squirrel had come down from a tree, dashed across the grass, and then up another tree. The Frenchie was desperate to chase it.

"Let me go, squirrel, need to stop it."

Lola pushed the thought out of her mind and tried to concentrate on the conversation. "Well, it's actually Tony I need to talk to you about. I'm working for Sandra Johnson, to find out if her husband could have been murdered."

The father's eyes narrowed and he nodded his head slowly. "I'm going to sound a little like Tilly now, for I really do hate to speak ill of the dead, but I can see many people would have a bone to pick with Mr. Johnson."

Lola nodded and let out a slight sigh. At least the father seemed prepared to help her.

"Let me go, they're plotting things," Sassy said, letting out a high-pitched whine as the squirrel hopped about in the branches. "It'll be your fault if I don't stop it."

Lola knew that her dog believed that squirrels were plotting to take over the world. At first, she had gone along with this, but now she realized she should have discouraged it from the start. It was too late now.

"I'm hearing that a lot, I'm sad to say," Lola said. "Could I ask you if Tony was with you Saturday and if so what time he was here?"

"Yes, Tony is a big help to me. He volunteers to keep the churchyard tidy and he was cutting the grass and the hedges for me on Saturday. Let me think... I believe he arrived around 11. I made him some lunch at one, he wasn't going to stop and I couldn't let him work without eating, I think he finished around 3.30, it could've even been 4. Does that help?"

"Yes, it does. I really didn't believe that Tony had done this but his alibi proves that he couldn't have. Thank you for your time, Father. If you can think of anything else that may help, please let me know."

"I know I shouldn't say this, but I know his ex-wife was… rather angry at her settlement. She had made threats in the past. Of course, many of us say things in anger and that doesn't mean that we would carry them through."

"She is on my list of suspects. I didn't know she had made threats."

"I really shouldn't have said anything but it is common knowledge and you would find out from someone else. Let me just say that Bethany is not a bad person, just a little insecure."

"Thank you, Father." That was a curious way to describe Bethany. She appeared so confident and so angry, how could he think she was insecure. Then Lola let her mind drift back to her career in the military and it all came together. Often, those who put up the bravest and most aggressive front were the ones who were frightened, or insecure. They decided that it was best to attack first hoping their enemy would back down at such a show of force. Could that be how Bethany felt? Could she be putting up a front to hide her real feelings?

It didn't matter, she was back on the suspect list.

"Any time, my child, I'm here to listen if you have other things to talk about."

The vicar's words brought Lola out of her thoughts, his perceptive eyes searched her face and Lola realized that he had seen her jump and must know that it was more than a normal startle. Maybe in time, she would think about discussing her past again, but not now. Healing had to take time.

For now, she would head back to see Bethany and see if there was anything else she could find out.

PAYMENT IN KIND

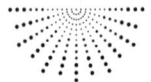

Lola arranged to meet Bethany at her home address. Quickly putting Sassy into the car they set off on the short journey. Lola was not quite sure what she expected but when she arrived outside the small semi-detached house it was not this. Bethany came across as somebody rich and special. Despite her anger, her clothing made her look a little bit above the rest. Lola had certainly felt inferior beside her.

The house was nice, well maintained, the garden a riot of color. Apricot nonstop begonias cascaded from pots and planters and over a small walled garden. Mixed in with them were Surfinias, lobelia, and others that Lola didn't recognize. The whole look was one of color and vibrancy. Apricot was obviously Bethany's favorite color.

Knocking on the door and clutching tightly to Sassy's lead Lola waited for Bethany to appear. Even though she had arranged the meeting, part of her didn't expect her to be here. Maybe she was a good suspect after all.

The door opened and Bethany appeared. Though her clothing was immaculate she was in a slim-fitting shift dress in a regal blue, her makeup however was a mess. Smears of mascara ran down her cheeks and her eyes were rimmed with red rather than black. She had obviously been crying for some time.

"Come on in, come on in," Bethany said and beckoned for Lola to follow her before dabbing at her eyes with a neat pocket handkerchief.

For a moment Lola had thought she had another suspect and a good one then it dawned on her. Looking down Lola noticed that even at home Bethany was wearing her signature 3-inch heels. The shoes were immaculately polished all shiny black with a little silver bow on top. Lola was pretty certain that Bethany would never be found dead without her heels. There was no way to get to the swim pond without going across the grass. The perfect grass with not a blade out of place. If somebody had gone over it in those heels it would have made holes in the turf. Apart from this, if Bethany had killed him on the rocks, where Lola thought it had happened, she would not have been strong enough to drag the man into the water.

Lola let out a sigh as another suspect bit the dust.

Bethany led her into a small sitting room. Like the rest of the place, it was immaculate. On the walls were pictures of stately homes and their gardens. Bethany sank down onto a grey velvet sofa with a sigh.

"I know, I know," she sobbed. "My Fred is gone and now I will get nothing."

Lola had to bite back a comment. A man was dead and all Bethany could think about was her own financial situation.

"Need to go sniff," Sassy said in Lola's mind. "To find clues."

Reaching down and trying not to draw attention to herself, Lola unclicked Sassy's lead and let the little bulldog go. Bethany hadn't noticed, she was too busy shaking her head and bemoaning her own situation.

"Do you have any news on the key?" Bethany asked. "I assume the contents of whatever, or wherever it is will be mine... oh, maybe it's a house... maybe my Fred finally came to his senses and bought me somewhere nice." Her eyes drifted up to one of the photos.

"I'm sorry, I don't have any leads yet but I am looking into it. I hate to say this but even when I find it... if it is anything of value then it would have to go into the estate and be distributed according to Mr. Johnson's will."

"No, Fred meant it for me or why would he have given it to me. I bet that shrew of his wife killed him. Maybe he was going to change his will and leave everything to me. Yes, I bet that was it. Maybe you can find proof and I can get what I'm owed."

Bethany had perked up at this new realization and was sitting with her head high, her shoulders squared.

"Good smells, but too clean," Sassy said as she wandered around grunting and grumbling. Sometimes she would sniff in and then blow the scent out as if she had to clear her nose before taking more scent in.

"I will continue to look into it," Lola said. Even though she knew Bethany was most likely not a suspect she still felt as if she should ask for an alibi. Of course, the woman could have hired someone but why would she? Unless she knew more about the key than she was saying there really was only one motive and that was jealousy.

Jealous people usually acted on impulse. It was not impossible that she sat down calmly and plotted her revenge but it didn't sit well with Lola.

"Oh, prize," Sassy said.

Lola glanced over to see that the Frenchie had disappeared into another room. Sending the thought of *what have you found*, she still tried to concentrate on Bethany.

"Continue," Bethany almost shrieked. "Are you telling me that you have had all this time and you haven't found out what it opens? How hard can it be?"

Lola wanted to say very hard but instead, she smiled. "I have some promising leads," she said instead and hoped that Louisa would be able to find something out about the key. It intrigued her and seemed to be the only thing that was out of place in Fred's life. "What can you tell me about Fred and about his behavior over the last few times you saw him?"

Bethany's eyes widened. "Really, do you think there is a clue in that?"

"There could be."

"Well, let me think. He was very passionate since we rekindled our relationship, but then he always was."

Lola didn't think that Fred was interested in a relationship. The man seemed like a real dog and a wrecker of more than homes but of lives. Instead of saying anything she smiled and encouraged Bethany to continue.

"Well, he gave me the key and smiled in that way that always made my heart miss a beat or two. It was as if he were sharing some big secret with me. As if we were in this together."

"Did he say anything, give any hint as to what that secret was?"

Bethany shook her head. "No."

"Did he take you out or mention anywhere he had been?"

Once more Bethany shook her head.

Lola wondered if they were going to get anywhere here and she knew she had to ask the alibi question but she was dreading it. "Do you have any thoughts as to what it was he was hiding with the key?"

"No, of course not. If I did I wouldn't have had to hire you... however, I'm beginning to think I hired the wrong person." Bethany shook her head and raised her nose as if to dismiss Lola.

With things going this well Lola decided she may as well ask the question and risk the woman's wrath. "I have to ask you, do you have an alibi for the time of his death."

"What!"

"I'm not insinuating that you had anything to do with it, but I do have to ask."

Bethany's eyes opened so wide they looked as if they would pop from her face. "You're working for me, not her."

"Well, actually, I'm working for her too. I took her case before I realized it had anything to do with you."

"Out, get out, you and that mangy dog. I don't ever want to see you again and you can return my key."

"Of course," Lola said sending a message to Sassy to get to her. "I don't have the key on me, I was looking into its origins but I will return it."

"I had a copy cut but if I find you stole what it unlocks I will sue you for every penny you have." Her eyes widened and a smirk came over her face. "Not that I imagine you have much."

Lola made her way to the door and clicked the lead on Sassy's harness. The Frenchie was keeping her head down as they left the house.

Lola let out a sigh as Sassy trotted before her back to the car. "I don't think she did it."

"Me neither, bitter smell but not dark," Sassy said mumbling her words.

"That's one job we won't get paid for," Lola said with a chuckle.

That was when Sassy turned to her and sat looking up so cute holding a pair of pink socks. The Frenchie had her payment.

Lola couldn't help but laugh.

A DEAD END

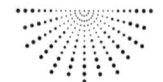

*L*ola was at a loss. She had eliminated all of her suspects and so she decided to go back to see Tilly.

Pulling up to the curb a short distance away she left the car, and she and Sassy made their way to the shop. Outside the shop, Lola could see a bunch of four lads leaning against the wall. They each had a can of cider and their heads were down until Lola got close.

"That's the ghoul who's trying to steal off my mum," Tyler said as he raised his head and Lola became aware of him.

Instead of contradicting him, which she knew is what he wanted, she just nodded and acknowledged him. "Hey,

Tyler, I'm sorry about your loss." Before he could do anymore, she walked into the shop heralded by the tinkling of the bell.

"How are you doing?" Tilly asked coming around from behind the counter. "Have you got anywhere with the case?"

Lola let out a sigh and shook her head. "I've been through all the suspects you gave me and I don't think it's any of them. It's still a possibility it could be Brent, that he could have hired someone, but I'm not convinced."

"It's quiet in here this time of the day, why don't we go in the back and have a cup of tea?" Tilly said. Not waiting for Lola to answer, she walked through the door into her private quarters.

Lola followed her and she and Sassy were soon sat down at Tilly's table.

Tilly busied herself putting on the kettle and putting loose tea into the teapot.

"Can you think of anyone else?" Lola asked, feeling a little bit of a failure that she hadn't been able to solve this herself.

"Well, there is of course Tyler's father. Brian Sharpe. I believe he was in the shop that first day you came in."

Lola thought back and then it struck her, that was where she recognized Tyler from. He was a spitting image of his father only Brian had seemed open and nice but Tyler seemed the opposite. The boy was closed up and though she hated to think it she felt he was bad to the bone as Tony had said. Admonishing herself for thinking so badly of him she remembered that he was grieving. Fred may not be his father, but he had been living as such, and for a boy that young to lose someone so close was not easy.

"Was the split amicable?" Lola asked.

Tilly came to the table, put down the teapot and 2 cups. Pouring a splash of milk into her own, she poured the tea through a strainer and then poured one for Lola. Before she sat down, she pulled a treat out of her pocket.

Sassy leaped off Lola's knee and was sitting in front of Tilly so quickly you could hardly see it.

"May she have this?" Tilly asked.

"I think she would gnaw my foot off if I said no," Lola said.

THE CASE OF THE MIX-UP MURDER

The treat taken, Sassy ran across the room and curled up to enjoy her prize.

"Now, where were we?" Tilly asked. "Yes, Brian Sharpe. Sandra and Brian had one child, Tyler, but he was always difficult. Always in trouble and I can't help but think that he didn't help in their marriage. Brian is such a lovely man, he can't do enough for anyone and Tyler is exactly the opposite."

"How did the marriage end?"

"I think it was Fred," Tilly said. "I think that Sandra was having an affair and Brian found out."

"And you think this gives him the motive to kill Fred?" Lola didn't know why she had asked that; of course, it gave him the motive to kill Fred. The man had stolen his wife, broken up his family. It was the oldest motive in the book.

"At the time I would've said so," Tilly said and shrugged her shoulders. "However, now he's been seeing a lady called Felicity Smith for quite some time. She's wonderful, if a little crazy, and the two of them, as far as I know, are very happy. Well, I know she's a bit upset because her cat went missing a few months ago. That's cats though, they do tend to stray."

"Yes, they do, do that." Something Bethany had said came back to Lola. "Did Sandra get a good settlement when they divorced?"

"I don't like to gossip, but yes, I heard she did take Brian to the cleaners. She kept Tyler, of course, but I'm not sure that Felicity would want him anyway." Tilly took a sip of her tea and shook her head. "I'm sorry I'm starting to gossip here, but I do hear a lot of things in the shop. You know me though, I don't like to say a bad word about anybody."

"Where would I find Brian?"

"Oh, that's easy. The main road going into Lincoln, your second on the left, he lives just down there and has a little shop next to the house called the Oak Barn. He makes furniture and beautiful it is too."

"I think I will head over to see him, but I don't know, maybe it isn't a murder."

"Let me cut you a slice of cake and then I want you to close your eyes while you're eating it and listen to what your instincts tell you. I really believe it's murder and that's not just because I'm excited about working on a case with you."

Lola laughed and did just as she was told. Although, as she bit into the cake and closed her eyes it was very hard to concentrate on anything but the deliciousness that was melting into her mouth. When she had finished, Tilly was right, she still believed it was murder and she knew she should follow her instincts.

As they left the shop, Tyler came and stood in front of her blocking her way. Lola could feel Sassy starting to bristle at her feet. "Easy, Sassy."

Tyler was up in her face. "You leave my family alone. If it was murder, it was that Munch Munch. We saw him there that day, didn't we?"

Nods and murmurs of agreement went around the crowd, but Lola knew that wasn't true for she knew that Tony had been over half a mile away at the local church.

"If it ain't him, then it's Brent. That fool was always jealous of Fred and he would do anything to get rid of him from the firm. So, go arrest one of those and leave us alone."

"Do you have any proof that it was Brent?" Lola asked without even realizing she had done it.

Tyler turned around to one of the boys. "Sam, tell her what you told me."

Sam was a mild-looking boy around 17 and just starting to grow some fuzz on his chin. His dark brown hair was spiked to perfection but his eyes wouldn't meet Lola's. It was as if he didn't want to say what he was going to say. However, he gulped audibly and pushed the words out. "I did see a man skulking around in the woods behind Tyler's house. He was stocky, and you know, a lot like Brent."

"There you have it," Tyler said. "Now, get out of here before I kick that mutt and show you what I think of you." Taking a step towards them his face screwed into a sneer.

Lola nodded. "Thank you for your help." With that, she walked away and found that Tilly was following her.

"I'm sorry about that," Tilly said.

"It's okay, I'm sure his behavior is just because of the grief."

"Well, if you're sure!" Tilly said. "I will see you soon."

As Tilly walked away Lola's phone rang and she answered it without looking. "Hello, Lola speaking."

"Hi, Lola, it's Louisa, Louisa Meeks I don't know if you remember me."

"Of course, I do, Louisa, how are you?"

"I'm good despite everything. I lost my job, though I thought I would do. Luckily, before I did, I managed to find something out for you. I have the details about the key for you if you still want them."

THE KEY

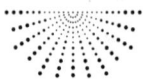

*L*ola felt a buzz of excitement. What could the key be hiding? "I'm so sorry to hear about your job but I'm sure you'll find something better soon, if you need a reference let me know."

"You would do that for me? Thank you so very much."

"Anytime, now, what is that key hiding?"

"I have no idea what's in it, but it is for a small box from a company called U-Store that is situated off Monks Road."

"That's excellent, do you know what I need to get access to it?"

"I rang them for you," Louisa said. "I told them that I was Fred's assistant and that I needed to come and clear out the box. They didn't ask for my name, and he said all I needed was the key. Do you want me to come with you?"

Lola shook her head though she knew Louisa couldn't see it. "No, that's fine, I will go on my own but thank you so much for your help."

"It's not a problem, if you ever need an assistant let me know. I think it would be fun working with you."

Lola wished she could give the young woman a job but at the moment her business just didn't warrant it. "I don't at the moment, but I will bear you in mind. You look after yourself and thank you again."

Lola typed the address into her phone and saw that it was not that far away. She decided she may as well go now, even though she had been sacked by Bethany, Sandra still deserved to know if there was anything incriminating in the box. Who knows, the contents of this box might blow the case wide open.

Louisa was right, the young man on the U-Store front desk with the black slicked-back hair, eyeliner, and an expression that could sour milk, wasn't interested in Lola's identity one little bit. It took him all his time to pull his eyes away from his phone. He took the key, looked at the number, and led her down a series of corridors. Then in front of them was a bank of multi-colored boxes, each with a number on. It didn't take them long to find box 256.

"I can wait for you or I can leave you to it, which would you prefer?" the young man asked.

Lola was sure he wanted to get back to playing the game on his phone that he was when she arrived so she told him to leave her to it. There were arrows on the floor which would help her find her way back. Anyway, she wanted to open the box in private.

A touch of excitement was bubbling inside of her and at her feet, Sassy sat and stared up all expectant.

"Will it have treats in?" Sassy asked, her little tongue lolling out in anticipation.

"I don't think so, well, not the sort of treat you're thinking."

Sassy let out a big groan and grumbling curled up on the floor.

Lola chuckled at the short attention span of her friend and opened the box. Inside, she found a large brown envelope. For a moment she wondered if she should go ahead and look. After all, she had been fired. However, she decided she could always go back and see Bethany and tell her what was there. In fact, she would do so anyway and not expect any payment.

With a shaking hand, not through nerves but with excitement, she reached in and pulled out the envelope. It was fastened with a metal clip that went through a hole and folded over. Straightening the two pieces of metal she opened the envelope and shook the contents into the box.

"Well, I never," she said for it was full of photos of Brent Burton with a selection of very young and very attractive ladies. No one in them was wearing a stitch of clothing and the girls looked as if they were barely legal. So it looked as if Brent was every bit as bad as his partner, only maybe a little more discreet. Was Fred blackmailing him? If so he had a definite motive to keep Fred quiet. However, would he have done it without getting the photos first?

The only thing these photos answered was that there was nothing for Bethany. Fred had simply been up to his old tricks and had been using his ex as nothing more than a booty call. For a moment Lola felt sorry for her, but it passed quickly, Bethany was just that sort of woman.

Putting the photos back in the envelope she decided the best thing to do with them was to give them to Wayne. There was little more pressure she could put on Brent, but maybe Wayne could. If nothing else, Wayne could get hold of Brent's financials. If the man had hired a hitman then surely there would be something in his finances that would lead them to the killer.

As Lola and Sassy wandered back down the corridor doors to leave the storage place, Lola began to wonder where she could look next.

Once in the car Lola and Sassy made their way back to the village. The evidence she had found was compelling but it got her nowhere. As she came over the hill and turned into the village the park was to her left and she saw Sam, Tyler's friend, walking through the gates. The boy had his head down and looked thoroughly miserable.

On impulse, she pulled into the car park and decided to go and talk to him. She wanted to find out why Tyler had lied. The boy was convinced that his father died accidentally and yet he was making up stories about seeing people lurking around the property. Could Brent have been there? It was possible. The man had the money to buy an alibi just as easily as he had to pay a hitman.

Lola pulled over and chuckled. When she moved to England she had expected it to be a quiet life. In fact, she had feared that she would be bored. Though she wanted a different environment, wanted to get away from anything that reminded her of her time in service, she still wanted intrigue... well, it looked like she had got exactly what she wanted.

The park was secure and an area where dogs were allowed to run and exercise freely. There was a large grass area surrounded by a Hawthorn hedge and in one corner a pond with benches around it. On the other side was the children's play area.

Sam had gone to the pond and was sat on one of the benches smoking. What was it with young people and cigarettes? Lola couldn't understand it, she thought they would have more respect for their bodies having been aware of the dangers before they started such a habit. Still, sometimes you have to learn the hard way.

"Birds, birds, look, birds," Sassy was straining on her lead, stood on her back legs and quivering with excitement as she looked across the field at two black ravens hopping around on the grass.

"They're bigger than you," Lola said.

"Feather, chase, run," Sassy said and then let out a high-pitched squeal which sounded a little like a baby pig being tortured.

Lola unclipped the lead, "Wait," she said and Sassy quivered even harder. Her muscles straining and her whole body was shaking in anticipation. "Okay," Lola said and the lilac bullet set off across the grass. Sassy hunkered down as she ran, her little legs going so fast she was almost a blur.

Lola had seen this play out many times, the birds would wait until the last minute and then launch lazily into the air. As always, Sassy got there just in time to run under their wings. She leaped into the air but missed by a mile. The two birds circled around her and then flew over the hedge, most likely landing on the other side.

Lola set off to walk over to Sam while Sassy checked the hedges, sniffing and searching for anything else she could chase.

With a chuckle, Lola pulled her eyes away from Sassy and back to Sam. The boy was still looking rather miserable, his shoulders hunched, his head down as he studied the ground. There was no can of cider now, the cigarette was gone, he had nothing and looked lonely and as if he needed a friend. Slowly, Lola crossed to him, coming at an angle so that he could see her approaching. At first, she thought he would walk away. She knew he was thinking about it but at the last moment, he shrugged and leaned back. His expression changed from one of despair to one of nonchalance. It was obvious that this was put on for her benefit.

"Hey, Sam, how you doing?"

"Okay."

Lola sat down at the opposite end of the bench to him. She said nothing just let the silence between them grow. Sassy came running up, her tongue hanging out, she was puffed, her eyes gleamed with excitement.

"Nearly caught the birdie". She flopped down at Lola's side and lay on the cool grass panting.

Lola noticed that Sam's eyes drifted across to the dog and there was a flicker of a smile on his face. "Do you like dogs?" she asked.

"They can be fun."

"This little one has been so great for me she helps me a lot." Lola noticed the interest in his eyes, he couldn't understand how a dog so small could be helpful. It was a stall. If she could get him curious then she could get him talking. Though she didn't understand why, instinct told her that this conversation was important. "I was in the military and in Afghanistan. My vehicle hit an IED and many of my friends were killed.

"That's really rad... I'm sorry."

Lola shrugged mimicking his nonchalant behavior. "It's okay, it was a few years ago. I don't like to admit this but I ended up having panic attacks. You know, if I heard a loud bang or if someone shouted. Little Sassy, here, she's been trained to recognize when I'm having an attack and she can help bring me back to the here and now. I can't believe how clever she is."

"May I stroke her?"

"Sure, she would love that."

Sam, got off the bench and down on his knees in front of Sassy. Pulling her onto his lap he stroked her head, and just behind her ears in the spot she loved most.

"You're a natural," Lola said.

Sassy was now lying on her back in Sam's arms while he rubbed her tummy. Her eyes were closed, her tongue lolling out, she was in heaven.

"I used to have a dog." The smile dropped off his face and his shoulders held the weight of the world once more.

"What happened?" Lola asked.

"It was a crossbreed, maybe Labrador and German Shepard. He was my friend, Max. Max went missing and we never found him."

"I'm sorry. That would break my heart."

He shrugged again but she knew that he was just putting on a face. "Why do you hang out with Tyler?" Lola asked.

Sam stood up lifting Sassy with him and sat back on the bench. The Frenchie was still in heaven being cuddled and petted. For a moment, Lola thought he wasn't going to answer. Then he shrugged. "You don't go against Tyler, not if you know what's good for you."

Lola understood, he needed a friend, someone who could help him get away from Tyler, from the bully. Well, maybe Sassy and she could become that friend, at least for a little while.

"If you ever want to walk with us I go out most nights at 17:00, you're welcome to join us."

"Yeah, I might. It would help keep you safe… after all, if there is a killer about you can't be too careful."

Lola nodded. "Thank you, I would appreciate that."

A smile came over his face and he seemed to relax for the first time in a while. Feeling as if she had got somewhere she pushed her luck. "I know Brent and Tony weren't at the Johnson house that day, why did you lie?"

Sam shuffled in his seat and dropped his head. "I didn't… I… I can't." Putting Sassy on the floor he ran off across the field like a rabbit who's seen the farmer's gun.

"Wow, fast," Sassy said. "He nice, me likes."

Lola had to agree but his recent behavior did make her wonder. Why had they lied?

THE SQUIRREL DID IT

*A*s Lola got back into the car her cell rang and she answered. "Hello, Lola speaking."

"Oh, hello, Lola, Miss Ramsey, it's Alice about the property that used to be the garage."

"Oh, hello, Alice, do you have any news for me?"

"Well, everything's going ahead as we expected but I've had a rather strange development."

Lola waited but realized that Alice wasn't going to say anymore unless she asked her. "Is it something I can help you with?"

"Well…"

The silence stretched and Lola realized that she had to wait. Alice was struggling with something and if she pushed her she may decide not to say. It was a technique she had learned in the military. People had to fill the silence and the best way to get someone to talk was often to say nothing.

"I believe the word has got around that I'm selling you the property," Alice said and Lola could hear her gulping as if she was worried.

"Well, I've had 4 people make me an offer, this afternoon. Obviously, I told them it's already sold. They also didn't want to offer as much as you but it just seems so strange."

Lola felt the same too. The property had been empty for some time, so why would 4 people want it at the same time as she did? "Do you know these people?"

"Well, they are a little rough, two of them used to work for my brother and the other two I only know by reputation."

"Do you want to tell me a little more about them?"

"Oh, no, I don't think I'd better. I just wanted to let you know that the property is yours and that I wouldn't back down on a sale. I don't believe in gazumping. If I hear any more I'll let you know, too da loo."

With that, she was gone and Lola wasn't sure whether to laugh or to worry. Obviously, something was going on here. However, it was something for another day. She didn't even have a name to ask Wayne about.

Back at the house, Tanya and Wayne were sat down to a Chinese takeaway.

"I got you a foo yung," Tanya said as Lola came in. "It's in the oven keeping warm."

Lola felt a flush of warmth and a feeling of such welcome that she was overwhelmed. "Thank you, thank you so much. I'll just feed the little one and then I'll sit down if you don't mind."

"We don't mind, do you want wine or beer?" Wayne asked.

"I'll grab a beer from the fridge, thank you."

Once Sassy had been fed Lola joined them at the table with her own meal. She suddenly realized how hungry she was and was so glad that she wasn't having to start cooking at this time of night. Once they had eaten and the table was cleared she could see that Wayne wanted to say something.

"I have some information for you too," she said.

Wayne chuckled. "The autopsy came back today. It is looking more like foul play. However, there's nothing that really gives us any help. The attacker was probably not massive but it's inconclusive. There were four blows, so it is unlikely that it was a sudden loss of temper. Whoever killed him was determined to finish the job."

"That's disappointing, I was hoping for something conclusive."

"Oh, Fred had been in a fight before he was killed. Punches to his ribs, damage to his throat. It was at least 8 hours before but the coroner can't narrow it down any further."

"Do you think this is related?" Lola asked.

"Knowing Fred it's not entirely impossible that two people wanted to put their hands on him... however, it would be a coincidence."

"Yeah, I see that."

"Can I offer any more help?" Wayne asked.

"Could it have been a woman?" Lola asked even though she didn't really have a female suspect at the moment. Something had made her ask that question and she wasn't sure why.

"Yes, the coroner did speculate that the death blows could be a woman, the punches to his ribs, the hands on his throat, less likely."

Tanya laughed. "This police work is really precise, so you're not looking for Arnold Schwarzenegger. Do you mind if I go paint?"

Lola and Wayne both chuckled. "Go ahead," Wayne said. "I'll join you in a little while."

"Are you thinking the wife?" Wayne asked.

"I guess it's possible but it wouldn't really make sense would it? After all, you guys had decided it was an accident. If it was her, the sensible route would've been to leave it well alone, and if she didn't beat him..."

Wayne took a long pull of his beer and leaned back. She could see that he was weighing up the evidence in his mind. "In many cases, the wife is the culprit... however, I think you're right. Did you say you had something for me?"

Lola nodded and brought out the envelope. Quickly, she filled him in on being hired by Bethany, the key, and the eventual finding of the photos. "I thought if I pass these to you, you might be able to put more pressure on Brent than I can. Personally, I don't think it's him but he does have a good motive and he does have the finances to pull this off."

Wayne pulled out the photographs and whistled as he looked at them. "Well now, Mr. Goody two-shoes had a secret or two of his own to hide. These girls look barely legal."

"Those were my thoughts; do we have him on anything here?"

"No, not without tracking them down and checking their ages. This looks consensual. I will run his financials if they haven't already been done. He is a good suspect. I hate to admit but he's one person I don't take to, he has this air of… superiority… but if he hadn't found these it would've been too risky to kill Fred with these out in the wild."

"That was my point too," Lola said.

"Do you have any more suspects?" Wayne asked.

THE CASE OF THE MIX-UP MURDER

Quickly, Lola ran through what she had investigated so far and she could see that Wayne was impressed by her thoroughness and her reasoning. It felt good that this professional valued her input and she was determined to help him as much as she could. Forgetting the obvious value of justice and finding the killer, who knew when she might need a favor down the road?

"I have a few other ideas but I want to go back and see Tilly."

Wayne chuckled. "I know what you mean, if something is going on our Tilly is sure to know. As much as I can, I'll keep you informed with what I find out if you will do the same?"

"Of course, I will, I will even let you make the arrest?"

Wayne chuckled.

"Should I give the photos to Bethany?" Lola asked.

"No, let us do it. You did the right thing in getting them but she might not see it that way. If you give me the key, I can tell her you handed it in and show her the photos. I don't need to mention that you had them first." With that, he said his good night before retiring to his room with Tanya.

It had been a good couple of hours since Sassy had eaten so Lola took her for a quick walk before retiring to bed herself.

"You sad," Sassy said as she curled up on the bed across Lola's knees.

Lola was sat up planning to read for a while. Closing the book on her Kindle she ran her hand across the little Frenchie's lilac head. Sassy groaned in appreciation. "I'm not really sad, I just wish I could work out who the killer was. Do you have any ideas?

"I think it was the squirrel," Sassy said before she drifted off to sleep on Lola's lap.

CAUGHT IN A DOWNPOUR

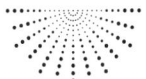

Lola showered and dressed in the morning and looked around the room for Sassy. The Frenchie seemed to be nowhere around. Quickly, Lola checked for her bed socks. They were gone, but the door was closed so Sassy couldn't have gone running off with her treasure.

Lola checked in the wardrobe and in the en-suite but the little dog was clearly hiding, hunkering down to enjoy her prize. Then she caught her out of the corner of her eye. Sassy was hiding under a chair, socks in her mouth with her paws over them. her little eyes bright, her tail quivering with excitement.

"Where is that little dog?" Lola said turning her eyes away and yet stepping towards the puppy. "If I don't find her soon I won't have time to feed her before we have to rush out. Now, where can she be?"

A muffled bark came from under the chair and Sassy ran out spitting out the socks to sit in front of Lola, her little tail wagging. "Me hungry."

"Oh, there you are," Lola said reaching down as if to stroke her, at the last minute she dove and grabbed the socks pulling them up, and then ran away with them. Lola threw them into the air and caught them as Sassy jumped up hoping that they would drop into her reach.

They raced back and forwards Sassy blocking her every move until Lola dropped to the floor laughing and let the bulldog pinch the socks. Sassy ran a lap of honor around the room and then dove on Lola.

"My socks, love the smell, my prize, lovey-lovey love love."

Lola laughed picking the little puppy up and removing the socks once more. She put them on top of the chest of drawers before leaving the room cuddling Sassy close. "You are a little monster," she said.

"But you love me," Sassy said licking her cheek.

"You bet I do."

"Morning," Tanya said. "Wayne has already left, I can do you some toast if you want some."

"That would be great," Lola replied. While feeding Sassy her phone buzzed. Lola dropped the dog food and it went all over the clean tiled floor. Sassy dove for the food. "Yummy in my tummy."

Lola almost tripped over her and grabbed for the phone but it was too late it had gone to voicemail.

"I'll clean up, sorry, Tanya." Lola left the phone, almost slipped on the kibble, and then almost stood on Sassy before she dropped to her knees.

"No need I can do it," Sassy said through a mouthful of kibble.

"Little piggy, there's twice what you normally get."

"So, it's good." Sassy was now snuffling down the food as quick as she could while Lola tried to pick up the excess. The kibble was rolling around the floor like a million brown marbles. Lola could have told Sassy to wait. The little dog was well trained and would have sat back down but she was having so much fun that it hardly seemed worth it. Luckily, Lola managed to get the majority of the excess up before the Frenchie could eat it all down.

"I smell Princess Portia," Sassy said as she wandered to the door. "Can I show her my socks?"

Lola stood up to see the pink socks that Sassy had stolen from Bethany in the bulldog's mouth. With a chuckle, Lola opened the door and Sassy trotted off down the garden to converse with the cat. Lola could only imagine what the rather aristocratic cat would think of them.

"That was exciting," Tanya said as she handed Lola the toast.

"The little Monkey-Moo certainly keeps me on my toes. How's your day going, are you visiting the gallery on the hill, if I remember right?"

"That's right." Tanya picked up her own toast and looked so delicate as Lola spread butter on hers and seemed to get more of it on the plate than the toast. "I'm going for a job there. I really want it and if I get it I will be in charge of bringing in new talent. There are to be some permanent artists and new ones each month."

"That sounds amazing and I know you will get it, you go show 'em, girl."

"I will." Tanya was finished and picking up her purse she left looking perfect.

Lola looked down to see she had spilled a bit of raspberry jam on her shirt and her fingers were sticky and greasy. With a sigh, she went to wash and change.

Once she was presentable again Lola checked her cell. There was a message from Sandra and she didn't sound happy. For a moment Lola thought about calling her back but then she decided it was best if she called around to see her. After all, the personal touch was always best.

It was just a short walk so she decided not to take the car. "Sassy, let's go walkies."

Sassy came running into the house her little tail up and wagging, still carrying the socks. "Where going?"

As Lola fastened on her harness she tried to think of where the case could go from here. Sam had given her things to think about, but nothing that could really lead her to the right person. Maybe Tilly could give her another suspect, but she felt a little bit as if she was failing by having to go back and ask the lady at the shop. There again, everyone needed a little help, sometimes.

"Princess Portia didn't like my socks," Sassy said.

"Really! I wonder why that is?"

"I think she wants Royal socks. Where can I get them from? Oh, they would be delicious, I wouldn't be sharing. Do you think Royal feet smell better?"

Taking the socks from Sassy Lola couldn't stop a chuckle. "I'm pretty sure all feet smell about the same. And I have no idea where we would get some Princess or Prince's socks. Maybe I can Google it later?"

"Me happy now, Royal socks."

As Lola and Sassy set off on the walk, she noticed there were clouds overhead. The recently bright blue sky was looking ominously threatening. For a moment, she considered taking the car. However, it didn't look as if it was going to rain anytime soon and it was only a short walk and Sassy did deserve to stretch her legs.

Within a few short minutes, they had made it to Sandra's and Lola knocked on the door.

"Oh, hello," Sandra said. "I think I've decided to stop all this nonsense. I think it was just my grief talking and I don't want to take this any further." Sandra started to close the door but Lola shook her head.

"I'm so sorry to hear you feel that way, Mrs. Johnson, unfortunately, it looks like this was a murder and so I can't really stop at this point. I'm sure you want to know the truth."

Sandra seemed to sag and it was only then that Lola noticed how exhausted she looked. It was not long since she had lost her husband and she was coping with a lot. It was understandable that she would have her emotions up and down and all over the place. There were deep bags beneath her eyes, her skin was sallow and seemed to hang on her face. She had lost weight and her hands fiddled with the cup she was holding. "I'm so sorry," Sandra said. "I had this strange idea that you were ripping me off, but maybe we should leave it to the police now?"

Sandra had opened the door and was walking through to the kitchen. Lola followed her and when she got there she found the two sons were sitting at the table. Connor's demeanor mimicked that of his mother. The boy was sad and exhausted and hardly touching the bowl of chocolate-looking cereal in front of him. Tyler, on the other hand, looked angry and jumped to his feet coming close and pointing a finger at Lola.

"When you gonna stop ripping off my mum? Just leave us alone, you freak, we want to... grieve in peace. No one's paying you another penny, you hear."

Sassy came and stood in between Lola and Tyler and gave a bark.

"Get that creature away from me or it's going in the pond?" Tyler said.

"Tyler, that's enough." Sandra stepped up as if to intervene. At the last moment she stopped, there was something strange about the look on her face. With that, she turned and ran from the room.

"Now look what you've done," Tyler said and stormed out after her.

Connor dropped his spoon onto the table and his head fell forward. The sound of sobbing could be heard.

"I'm so sorry you had to hear that," Lola said and wandered around towards him. Sassy was with her and reached up her paw and touched his leg. He looked down.

"I just miss my daddy so much."

"I understand, I lost my parents too. I know how much it hurts but it will go away in time."

Connor looked up his soft brown hair framed his face and big chocolate eyes looked through a pool of sadness. "Does it really go away?"

Lola thought about her own sadness and guilt. When her parents died in a road accident she had been deployed. It was awful, not that she could have done anything but still, she felt awful for things that were said and that she wasn't there. It was why she had never touched the money they left her. Only now, was she thinking of using some of it to buy the property and to have it worked on to make it livable. She had some of her own savings but not enough for this and as a good friend, Melody and her cute French Bulldog, Smudge, had once told her, her parents would want her to use the money. To use it for a good purpose and if she had a solid home and business premises then she could help a lot of people.

"There will come a time when you remember the good times when remembering is a joy for the life you shared together."

"Really?" The little boy's lip was shaking and he was trying so hard to hold back his tears.

"Really, why don't you tell me a good memory of your dad?"

Connor stared at her for a moment and then his eyes seemed to clear and a smile came on his face. "He was the best at storytelling. The one with the dragon, he always became a dragon and roared at me, and then he would be the little mouse creeping around. The mouse tripped up the dragon and they became friends. I love that one."

"That sounds amazing, I wish I'd heard it."

Connor jumped up. "I will lend it to you," he said racing from the room.

Sassy followed him and Lola stood alone in the kitchen wondering where this was going.

Connor came back in and showed her the book. It was large and full of lovely pictures and they read a bit together. Then he slumped back into the chair. "Was my dad murdered?"

Lola wondered what to say, whether it was even her place to do so and she was still struggling when he spoke again.

"I don't think my daddy fell, he wouldn't, he was so strong. I think it was a mix-up murder, no one would want to kill my dad. It was all just a mix-up."

Lola nodded, not knowing what else to say. Luckily she was saved.

Sassy came trotting back into the kitchen proudly holding a pair of red and black Superman socks.

Connor pointed at Sassy and let out a loud laugh while covering his mouth with his other hand. "She stole Tyler's socks, oh, they stink," he said giggling and holding his nose before chasing after the Frenchie. Sassy loved this and jumped and skipped around the room her head held high with her smelly prize.

Lola left them to it for a moment enjoying the boy's relief from sadness. "Swapsies," she eventually called.

Sassy grumbled in her mind but trotted over and sat in front of her. Lola swapped the socks for a treat and handed them to Connor.

"They are damp," Connor said and giggled. "Will you find the truth for me?"

"I will."

Connor looked at the socks and giggled again as he ran out of the room.

Lola decided it was time to leave. "You really must stop pinching socks."

"Why?"

"Because it's wrong."

"They so delicious. Boy's room smell of funny smoke and something else, I can't quite get a good sniff."

"I'm not surprised," Lola said. As they left the property, Sandra was sat by the swim pond; she looked so lonely and in so much pain. Lola hoped she could bring her some peace. For a moment she wondered about what Connor had said, a mix-up murder. Could it have been a mistake? Then she remembered Wayne telling her that there had been four blows to Fred's head. No, this was a cold-blooded murder and they were going to find out who was to blame.

BARELY LEGAL

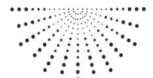

*A*s Lola and Sassy made the short walk towards Tilly's shop the day got darker. Lola looked up to see black threatening clouds rolling across the sky. The sun had gone behind them and there was a welcome breeze in the air.

"Smells like rain," Sassy said.

"It looks like it's going to rain too," Lola said. "You want to run home?"

Trotting along in front of her, Sassy shook, it was as if she was shaking off the water that hadn't fallen yet. "No, don't mind wet."

Lola wasn't sure whether she minded it, but it was almost as far to go home as it was to go to the shop. Increasing her pace, she decided to just get there a little quicker. A rumble of thunder sounded behind them and almost immediately the heavens opened. The rain came down fast and heavy. Lola was surprised that it was warm and not cold. For all she had heard about England it was much warmer than she had expected. Quickly, she set off in a trot. Sassy knew where they were going, with her ears down and her head lowered she pushed through the rain. The Frenchie galloped ahead and Lola was struggling to keep up. They arrived at the shop just as a flash of lightning lit up the sky.

Lola opened the door and burst through to find Tilly standing almost in the entrance. Slamming on the brakes she came to a rocking halt coming very close to knocking Tilly over.

"Oh, my, I guess it's raining out there," Tilly said as she peered through her glasses and wrinkled her little nose. "I was just coming to have a look out the window. It sounds pretty nasty, would you two like a cup of tea and a towel?"

"That would be lovely," Lola said.

Tilly set off down one of the aisles and pulled a package from the shelves. "Follow me."

Lola and Sassy followed her into the back room and found her pulling open the packet. Inside was a pink drying coat, a little bit large for Sassy but perfect for what they needed. Lola realized she didn't have her purse with her and her cheeks flushed. "Tilly, I am so sorry I came out without a cent."

"I do love your accent," Tilly said. "It reminds me of my holidays many, many years ago. But now don't you worry, I just thought this would be a great idea. I only started stocking them this year so it will be nice to see how it looks." She reached behind her and handed Lola a towel. "You sit down and dry yourself while I dry this little one."

"Towlie, towlie," Lola called to Sassy and the little Frenchie came up to her. Lola pointed at Tilly holding the pink coat and Sassy trotted across excited to have one of her favorite things. The little dog might not always like getting wet but she always loved getting dried.

While Tilly put the towel over Sassy and then rubbed her down through it, Lola could hear her grumbling and groaning her delights while she dried off her own hair. Tilly was laughing and thoroughly enjoying herself as Sassy squirmed beneath her fingers. Once she was done, she put the coat on the little Frenchie and fastened the Velcro beneath her. It was so cute with a little hood to keep her ears warm.

"Now, let me make that tea."

Soon they were drinking tea and sat around the table. There was some chocolate shortbread for Lola and a gravy bone for Sassy.

"How are you getting on with the case?" Tilly asked.

Lola was pleased she had asked for it made it easier for her to broach the subject of new suspects. Quickly she filled Tilly in. "So, there we are, I'm out of suspects and so many people have a motive, and yet I don't believe it's any of them."

"There is one more person it could be," Tilly said. "I believe we spoke about him briefly before and that's Tyler's father, Brian Sharp."

"Why do you think he could be a suspect?" Lola asked.

"Well, Fred cheated with his wife and stole her from Brian. That was why they got divorced. Fred also got

Sandra an amazing lawyer. They lied about the affair and Sandra got a very good deal. For a long while, Brian was almost bankrupt. That had to hurt."

"Yes, you are right, he is a good suspect. But there must've been a reason that you didn't mention him before."

"Ahh, well, if this had been three years ago or earlier, he would've been my first suspect. He was angry and hurt, not sleeping well, not eating, in a really bad place for a long time. Financially, his life was in ruins and his wife had custody of Tyler. However, that last bit is not necessarily a bad thing."

Tilly had said a lot and Lola took her time to sift through it. Tilly thought he could've done it before but she wasn't sure now, why? Why was not having his son not necessarily a bad thing? "So, what has changed?"

"He has an amazing new woman in his life, Felicity Smith. It's supposed to be secret but I found out about it and she is just perfect for him."

Lola was intrigued. "Tell me more about Felicity." Could the other woman have done it?

"Oh, Felicity is just a ball of sunshine. She is not as attractive as Sandra, a little more down to earth and I imagine a little less demanding. The two of them have been together now for a little over three years. I think it's getting serious and they will come clean about it soon. Many people know, if I'm honest, but Brian likes to think it's still a secret."

"Why would he want to keep it a secret if they have been together for so long?" That would surely upset Felicity, maybe she was a good suspect?

"I think it's because of Tyler. The reason I said about Tyler is that Felicity doesn't like him... oh, you know how I hate to speak badly of people, but does anyone?"

Lola nodded her agreement for she could understand the sentiment, but she wanted to find out more about Felicity. If she thought that Sandra was fleecing Brian then she had a good motive. And Lola knew that a jealous woman was not something to be toyed with.

"Is there a reason why Felicity doesn't like Tyler?"

Tilly shook her head and took a big sip of her tea. Then she pushed her glasses back up her nose and wrinkled that nose as if she was peering at something intensely. "Felicity blames him for her cat."

"Her cat!" Lola was confused.

"I believe he went missing. A big ginger Tom. It was such a shame," Tilly said as she took a sip of her own tea.

It seemed Tilly had drifted off the conversation for she spent the next 10 minutes talking about the ginger cat and how it used to come to the shop and she would feed it a sprat.

Lola decided she might need to talk to Felicity but she was not sure. Something else was nagging at the back of her mind but she couldn't quite put her finger on it. "Do you have any more information about Brent Burton?" Lola asked.

Tilly shook her head as if to pull herself out of the past. "A bit of a smarmy one that one. He puts on one face for the public and I'm sure he's something totally different in private. I did hear he had some dealings with a street gang, but I'm not sure how true it was. Sometimes they come around here. Luckily, they don't cause me any trouble. They also don't realize how thin these walls are." She chuckled to herself and took a bite of the shortbread.

"Did you know about his..." Lola wasn't sure how to describe the girls she had seen in the pictures. If they were of legal age they were only just and she didn't want to shock Tilly or disturb her too much.

"Oh, if you mean the girls he takes to the hotel on Ridgewood Road, yes, I know all about them. One of the mothers comes in here regularly. She's a real nice lady and I helped her get her Sarah out from under Brent's clutches. Fortunately, Sarah was of legal age. I must be an awful person because part of me wishes I could speak to one of the ones that weren't. I would like to see that man behind bars."

"How many other people know?" Lola asked before glancing across to see that Sassy had finished her biscuit and was sitting in front of the stove in her pink blanket. She looked incredibly cute.

"Not that many," Tilly said. "The man was discrete and used his money to pay off those he needed to. I think he was also into drugs. There was a rumor… oh, you are going to be mad with me now. There was a rumor that they were running them out of the garage at one time."

"Really," Lola said. "Do I need to worry about it?"

"No, it was over five years ago, then it was only a rumor."

For a few moments, they drank tea and nibbled on the shortbread. It was Tilly who broke the silence, "do you like Brent for this?"

Lola thought about it for a few moments. Part of her did, but part of her thought it was too messy. Brent was meticulous and if he had done this, then surely, there would only have been one blow. "I don't think so," Lola said, "but I can't rule him out just yet. I think I should go see Brian, just remind me how to get there."

"Oh, that's easy," Tilly said. "Take the main road going into Lincoln, your second on the left, he lives just down there and has a little shop next to the house called the Oak Barn, he makes furniture, and beautiful it is too."

Lola had two new suspects and Brent was back in her sights. Was she ever going to solve this case?

THE NEW WIFE

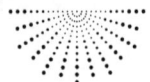

Lola made the short walk home and then, strapping Sassy into the car, she set off to visit Brian. She could remember seeing him when he came into the shop on her first visit there. Though it had only been a passing glance, she remembered he looked so happy. The smile on his face certainly didn't make her think of a killer.

Pulling the Jeep up to the side of the road she could see that he worked out of a converted garage and sure enough, Oak Barn was proudly displayed above the door.

It was the smallest semi-detached house in a nice enough neighborhood but nowhere near as nice as the village of South-Brooke. The garden however was amazing. It was full of color on one side with flowers of every color in the rainbow and every size and height. It was beautiful and drew her eye. As she scanned across to the other side of the garden it was laid to a vegetable plot. She could see beans and tomatoes, onions, and peas, and even some squash. Amongst the row of the beans, a woman was harvesting the bounty. She had a knife in one hand and a basket in the other and was slicing off the beans and dropping them into the basket. Though she had her back to Lola, she presumed this was Felicity.

Long brown hair touched with grey and a little bit straggly, it hung down her back. She was incredibly thin but also looked strong. Wearing denim shorts and a blue T-shirt, her legs and arms were tanned to perfection.

Clipping the lead onto Sassy's harness Lola climbed out of the car. The door to the Oak Barn was shut so she decided to go and introduce herself to Felicity. What was the best way to do that?

Wandering into the garden she called out, "Are you Felicity?"

The woman turned around and smiled. Tilly had been right; she certainly was a blast of sunshine for that smile just filled Lola with joy. It was genuine.

"Yes, I'm Felicity, how can I help you?"

Lola suddenly felt uncomfortable. However this went she was going to hurt this woman. After all, she was working with Brian's ex-wife and that had to hurt.

"Don't worry, I'm the pick," Sassy said trotting ahead of Lola.

"The pick?" Lola whispered hoping that Felicity wouldn't realize she was talking to the dog and call people from the funny farm to take her away.

"To break the ice," Sassy said and with that, she yanked on her lead and ran up to Felicity.

Felicity put down the basket and pulled Sassy into her arms covering her with kisses and hugging her close. "Well, aren't you a little sweetie?"

"I'm so sorry about that," Lola said as she arrived at her side. "I think she likes you."

"It's no problem, I love all animals especially dogs and cats. If only I could have one again!" Felicity put Sassy down and there was a sad look in her eyes but Lola couldn't quite place it. Maybe it was too painful after she had lost her last cat. Maybe it was too painful to get another.

"I hate to do this to you but I'm working for Sandra Johnson." Lola cringed waiting for the smile to be wiped from Felicity's face.

"Oh, yes, I'm so sorry to hear about Fred." A shudder ran through Felicity as if she was cold, but she put a smile back on her face. "Do you want to speak to Brian about it?"

Lola nodded. Felicity definitely seemed genuinely sorry about Fred. There was no hint of jealousy and as Lola looked around the garden she understood why. Felicity loved what she had and she was happy. But why had she shuddered? Something was going on, if only she could work it out. "Yes, if you don't mind, is he in the…"

"In his workshop, yes, he is, let me take you through, and would you like a drink of tea or coffee or something cool?"

"Thank you for the offer, but I just came from Tilly's and…"

"Oh, I guess you're full of cake and tea then, Tilly is certainly a good host. Come on, it's this way and Brian won't mind talking to you." Felicity led her through the garden and around the back of the house. Looking through the window she could see it was a home, a real comfortable, lived-in home. Flowers decorated nearly every room and there were pictures on the wall, memories. She could only see a little bit but somehow she knew that this couple was happy.

Felicity knocked on a side door and walked into the workshop. Brian was leaning over a piece of wood, sanding with long meticulous strokes, totally absorbed with his work. As the door opened light fell across him and he looked up. The smile that crossed over his face told Lola all she needed to know. He was totally in love with Felicity.

Brian kissed Felicity on the cheek.

"Oh, I'm sorry, I didn't get your name," Felicity said.

"I'm Lola. Lola Ramsey."

"Ahh, the American lady," Brian said. "I heard you were a Private Investigator... Oh," the smile fell off his face but only for a moment, "are you working for Sandra?"

"I'm sorry, but I am," Lola said. "She believes that Fred was murdered and I just wanted to ask you a few questions."

"Well, I totally understand but I swear I didn't do anything. Don't get me wrong, there was a time when I would've gladly throttled that man."

"Negative energy is not a good thing," Felicity said and reached out to touch his arm.

"I know, my love, I don't dwell on it anymore. We were away that weekend if that helps," he said turning back to Lola.

"Yes, of course, it does. Did you go anywhere nice?" She also wanted to ask if anyone had seen them but like most of the suspects, something told her that Brian or Felicity were not murderers.

"We went up to the Lake District, staying at a little bed-and-breakfast we stay at regularly. It was a lovely weekend away walking, but my, did it rain."

"Rain, urgh," Sassy said and shook herself as if she was shaking off the last of the water.

"Oh, gosh, yes," Felicity said and pulled out her phone. "Here, look at the pictures of us soaked." Felicity flicked through the pictures that were grey from the clouds in the constant rain. Both Felicity and Brian were soaked through to their skin but even so, on every photo, their smiles were bright enough to chase back the rain.

Lola knew she should probably ask for the details of where they had stayed but she didn't think she needed to. These two were not her killers.

"I want to thank you so much for your time and I really am sorry to have bothered you," Lola said.

"It's no bother," Felicity said. "Do you like beans or leeks?"

"Yes, I like both of them," Lola said confused.

"Excellent, let me get a carrier and I will get you some to take home," Felicity said before wandering off.

Lola looked at Brian for a moment then he smiled. "I understand why you had to come. I don't hold it against you. Looking back with hindsight, Fred did me a favor, I am happier than I could ever believe possible."

CASH FOR WHAT

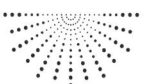

Lola sat in the car with Sassy on her lap. The Frenchie was alternating from kissing her ears and bouncing at the window every time she saw a bird. She never hit the glass but her whole body shook in the anticipation of chasing down what she called the black evils. The black birds ranged from blackbirds, through the bigger crows to the huge ravens. Sassy would chase them all and it worried Lola; after all, some of them seemed bigger than she was.

In the passenger footwell were two carrier bags bursting with greens. Felicity had added tomatoes and cucumber to the leek and beans. There was so much that Lola knew they could never eat it but what could she do with it? Felicity was so eager to share that she couldn't turn her down.

On the case, she was at an impasse once more, but an idea was forming in her mind. Before she could give it much thought her phone rang, it was Wayne.

"Hi, Lola, I looked into Brent's financials. A large sum of money was withdrawn two weeks ago. It could be nothing; in fact, he draws out a large sum on a regular basis. Always cash and I can't find anything legitimate to correspond with the payments."

Lola thought she knew what they were for, she shuddered. That was a case for another day and with Tilly's help, she would come back to that. Lola explained to him what she had been up to.

"I know where they go when they go away," Wayne said. "I don't see it being Brian or Felicity, I've never known two people more in love... don't tell Tanya I said that." He finished with a deep chuckle.

"I won't. What about Sandra Johnson?" For some reason, Lola kept being pulled back to the family.

"She said she was shopping but Fred was a real ladies' man and that had to hurt. I can run her credit card and get my constable to look over the CCTV. I'll let you know if we find anything."

"Great, Wayne, thanks. I'll be in touch." She didn't mention her theory but did say she might want to call on him later.

"No problem, I'm in the office all day tidying up some paperwork for one of my old cases. Call me if you need me."

Lola had an idea of what to do with the veggies, and hopefully to get some new perspective on her case. "Let's go see Tilly," she said.

Sassy barked her joy and taking one last look out the window she hopped across into the passenger seat. Lola clipped her harness onto the seat restrainer before starting the Jeep.

Soon they were pulling up outside Tilly's shop again. Once more, Tyler and his gang of ruffians stood in the corner. Lola clipped Sassy onto her lead and stepped out from the car. Her eyes drifted across to the boys in the corner. They were smoking, and from the smell, it was probably cannabis. There were also cans of cider scattered around their feet.

"That's that freak that's robbing my mum," Tyler said.

The gang of youths all turned and stared at Lola. It was just like a scene out of a zombie film. The undead had heard a noise, as one they turned, their eyes latching onto Lola. Any minute now she expected them to let out a brutal roar and chase her down. Knocking her to her feet and feasting on her flesh until she became one of them. Lola shook her head, maybe she'd been watching too much TV recently. A chuckle escaped her as the youths turned back to their master. They were just kids, and that's what kids were like.

Lola grabbed the two carrier bags from the wheel of the car and walked into the shop. She could see that Tilly was serving a customer. It was a woman she didn't know. She was in her 70s, with long grey hair that had once been black pinned up high on her head. There was something strong about her and she smiled kindly before turning back to Tilly.

Tilly rang up the items out of the woman's basket. "That'll be £32.96."

The woman handed over some cash and waited for her change. "You take care, Mrs. Summers," Tilly said as the woman left the shop.

"Hey, Tilly," Lola said. "I've got a bit of a quandary. I was given all of this by Felicity. There is no way that me, Tanya, and Wayne can eat all this, so I wondered if you know of anyone in need that I could pass it on to?" Just as she'd said the words Lola realized she should've taken it to the church. If she had been back home she would've had a much better idea of what to do with it and now she felt quite silly. Tilly's business was selling such produce, why would she give it away?

"Yes, I know just the people that would love to have this," Tilly said. "They are all pensioners, and no longer able to do their own gardens. Some of them are having to count their pennies too. Don't you worry, I'll make sure it gets to the people who need it."

"Thank you so much, Tilly," Lola said.

"I can't leave the shop at the moment, not while those boys are outside but I do have some lemonade if you would like a drink?"

"No, thank you, I'm fine." Lola was wondering how to broach the subject that she was stuck again. It seems ridiculous that the Private Investigator, the supposed professional, was having to ask the lady at the local shop. Maybe she wasn't as good at this job as she thought she was.

"How did it go with Brian and Felicity?" Tilly asked.

"They were away for the weekend, I haven't checked their alibi but I'm pretty sure I don't need to. I would bet my house that they are not the killers."

"I totally agree with you. And isn't she just lovely?"

Lola nodded. "I'm a little worried about Sam and I don't see him out there with Tyler at the moment. What do you know about him?"

"His mum lives on the estate just as you are going to town. She's a good woman, but she's overworked, tired, and not always there. Sam's a great kid. There's not a nasty bone in his body, he's just got himself in over his head and he doesn't know how to get out of it. If he is not here, I would imagine he's at that pond on the playing field."

"I saw him there yesterday. I think he really likes Sassy."

Hearing her name Sassy gave a little bark.

"Oh, my little love, I'm so sorry I've been ignoring you," Tilly said as she reached under the counter and then came around to the other side and handed Sassy a gravy bone.

The little Frenchie spun around twice and then curled up on the floor munching on her treat.

"You spoil her," Lola said.

"That's what they're there for, a little bit like grandchildren."

"Do you have grandchildren?" Lola felt a little guilty for not asking Tilly about her family on previous visits. She must be careful, was she getting so selfish that it was all about her and what she needed?

For the first time since she'd met her, Tilly's eyes clouded a little. "No, I was never able to have children." Then she smiled brightly. "But I've helped a lot of them. I sponsored 30 children over the years and I do bits for all sorts of charities. Listen to me going on like a silly old lady, you didn't come here to hear my tales, do you have any of the clues?"

"I do have an idea, I think Sam may know more than he wants to say. I just have to see if I can get him to talk to me."

"He's just scared. If he saw the killer or knows something he will tell you as long as you treat him with kindness and respect."

Lola felt that excitement deep inside her. The one that told her that she was on to something. The one that had driven her to become a Private Investigator and that made her look forward to every day, and every new adventure. Now all she had to do was coax a frightened young man to do the right thing. If Sam had seen something, she had to find out what. Had he seen the killer? Could they link that killer to Brent? The more Lola thought about it, the more she believed that Brent Burton had a lot to answer for.

AN EVIL TRUTH

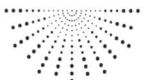

Lola found Sam exactly where she thought he would be, he was sitting on the bench next to the pond skipping stones across the water.

"Hey, Sam," she said as she sat down. She let Sassy go over to the boy.

"Hey," he said but then a big smile came across his face as he saw Sassy sitting and staring up at him. Scooping her up he lifted her onto his knee and snuggled his face into hers. "Does she like playing fetch?"

Lola laughed. "She does for a while, but she'd much rather run around with the ball and have you chase her."

"May I?"

Lola nodded.

Sam put her on the ground and pulled a ball from his pocket and waved it in front of Sassy's face. Her ears were immediately high and proud on her head, her eyes locked on the ball following it. Jumping in the air she gave a big bark and then spun around in a circle. Sam laughed and ran behind the bench with the ball throwing it.

The ball landed a long way from him and Sassy tore after it. Her little legs running so fast, her head down, her nose pointed. Sam tried to give chase, but despite her little legs, Sassy was fast. When she reached the ball, she grabbed it and twisted around on the spot trotting off with her prize.

"Sassy, Sassy, come here, girl," Sam shouted.

For a moment Lola thought Sassy would not come back. In her mind, she had fought hard for that ball. She had outrun the long-legged human and she deserved the victory. However, she was also great at reading people and she knew that Sam needed a friend. Turning on the spot she trotted back to him and sat in front of him dropping the ball at his feet.

Lola watched the boy play with the dog for around 10 minutes. The more they interacted the happier he became. It was as if the years and the worry were dropping off his shoulders and soon, he was laughing like a child again. It did Lola good to see it. She knew how much Sassy had helped her. At one time, any raised voice, any loud noise, and she was a quivering mess. With Sassy at her side she had been able to face most of her fears.

At last, the little Frenchie came back and slumped on her belly with her back legs stretched out behind her and the ball still in her mouth. Sam ran over following her and dropped down on the grass beside her.

"Do you have any water for her?" he asked.

Lola had already pulled the bottle out of her purse and the little fold-up dish that she always carried. Sassy accepted the drink gratefully. "He's fun," she said in Lola's mind.

"You're welcome to come and play with her, anytime you want," Lola said.

"Really!" Sam looked up his eyes were wide he smiled brightly and then a cloud passed over his expression. Suddenly, he had realized it would not be cool.

"Well, we can always meet here every now and again," Lola said.

"I would like that."

He sat on the grass stroking Sassy as they spoke. Lola hated to do it but she knew she had to bring things back to the murder. Hopefully, she had enough good graces with Sam that he would help her.

"Sam, what do you know about Brent Burton?"

Sam's shoulders drooped and his head dropped low as he avoided her eyes. "I think he killed Fred."

Lola was surprised by that and also surprised by the change in attitude. There was more going on here than she knew. "Why did you say that?"

"We saw him behind the house on that day, you know we did." Sam was still staring at the grass and subconsciously rubbing Sassy between the ears.

"You already told me that wasn't true."

Sam shrugged. "The man's a creep but worse than that, he's cold, hard, just the sort of person that would do this."

"He has an alibi," Lola said. For a moment she thought that Sam would go, that he would get up and run. Every fiber of his body seemed to tense, and she knew that she would not be able to catch him. But just as she thought he would go, he let out a big sigh, his whole body relaxed, and she was sure that she heard him let out a sob.

Her instinct was to get down there and hold him, after asking what was wrong, but she knew that was the wrong thing to do. This boy wasn't used to kindness from adults. She knew his mum was good and did her best, but she imagined that most adults he met on a day-to-day basis thought he was trouble. No doubt he had been getting into trouble for a lot of years and all he saw was authority. So instead, Lola left it to Sassy.

The little Frenchie was no longer lying on the ground. As Sam began to cry, she curled up onto his lap and cuddled in close to him, offering as much comfort and support as she could. Lola kept still and silent and waited for the little dog to do her work. Now, she was more intrigued; was he afraid of Brent, had he seen something that had upset him this badly? What could it be?

Sam wrapped his arms around Sassy and held her close as he cried. After a few minutes, he wiped away his tears and lifted his head staring straight at Lola. "I think he's my dad."

That was not what Lola had expected to hear and it took her by surprise. "What makes you think that?"

"My mum has a picture of them together from when she was young. She won't ever hear a bad word about him and sometimes I think I look a bit like him. My jaw, my cheekbones."

"Did you ask your mum?" Lola asked.

"Yeah, she told me to leave it alone. I guess that says it all, really. He lives in that fancy house, with everything, and my mum has to work two jobs..."

"Have you ever thought about approaching him?" Lola asked.

"I did approach him. The first time he offered me a thousand pounds to go away and never come back. I thought about it... but that's just like a new iPhone. It doesn't actually mean anything." A single tear was sliding down his face and he turned away brushing at it with his hand.

"That's a good way to look at it. You said the first time?" Lola was worried now, she didn't want to push him too far and yet she knew she had to hear this. She made herself a promise that once this case was over, if Brent wasn't in jail, she was going to start and look into him.

"I've contacted him about four or five times now. The first two times he offered me money and then he started to get a bit nasty. He said that kids can fall and break their legs, sometimes even their necks. It didn't scare me, but he threatened my mum, said she would lose her job, or worse. I kept away after that... but I did see him at Fred's two days before he died. He didn't know I was there, no one did."

Lola waited, but he seemed to not want to say anymore. Yet somehow, she knew this was important. If she was going to crack this case, she had to get this young man to talk. "I think that Brent used a lot of women, and probably still does. How old was your mum when you were born?"

Sam blushed and looked down at his hands stroking between Sassy's ears. "She's a really pretty color, I've never seen a dog this color before."

"She's called a lilac French Bulldog. Her coat is actually a pale greyish-brown color but it looks lilac, they also call it Isabella. At one time I was going to call her Bella because of it."

Sam chuckled. "Sassy suits her better."

Sassy sat up and licked his face.

"I think she agrees with you," Lola said. "Her full name is Sassy Pants."

Sam let out a peal of laughter and rolled over onto his back which delighted the little Frenchie. She lay down on top of his chest her back legs pointing out behind her, her nose inches from his, and then she burped.

Sam laughed even harder. Lola had to smile, that little dog always knew how to bring people out of a bad situation. Sam laughed until he was crying and then he sat up, hugging her, and turned to Lola. "She had just turned 16."

Lola held back a gasp, she had been right. If Brent really was Sam's dad then they had proof that he was sleeping with an underage girl. "I will help you find out the truth," Lola said. "Did you hear something between Fred and Brent?"

"It was the main reason I went ahead with what Tyler said, you know, to tell people that I'd seen him there. They were arguing about some pictures. It was full-on screaming at each other and I've never seen adults do that before. I filmed a little bit on my phone, but I was so shocked it took me a while to think to do it."

"Can you tell me about this?"

Sam froze. "I don't know, I'm frightened."

THE VIDEO

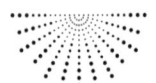

"You really should tell me, maybe I can help, but I won't know unless I know what you heard. I can be discrete, and I will keep you safe," Lola said.

Sam was looking back down at Sassy; he nodded his head as if in agreement and slowly looked up. "Okay." Reaching into his pocket he pulled out his phone and scrolled through until he found the video. "You may as well look at this first."

Lola came across and peered at the phone. Half of the picture was covered by a doorframe, the other half was the Johnsons' kitchen and she could see Fred pinned against the cabinets by a man. As he turned, she could see it was Brent. The view of him was small and a little blurred as the camera shook in Sam's hands. It didn't matter, she recognized his profile, the short greying hair, but mostly it was the air of the man. There was an arrogance, a belief he was above everyone, and looking at this that included his partner.

"Any more scandal and you're dead," Brent screamed at him while placing his hands around his throat and squeezing tightly.

Even on the small screen, she could see that Fred's eyes bulged and his face was red. It looked as if he was choking, then something happened, Brent was pushed back, letting go of Fred. Even through his gasping for breath Fred smiled and lowered his knee. It looked like he had raised his knee, right into Brent's happy sack and Brent doubled over backward. A chair went flying across the room and the two scuffled coming closer to the door. The phone was quickly pulled back, the picture lost for a few moments and even more shaky. When it steadied, you could see even less but you could still hear them.

"Scandal, I cause a scandal?" Fred shouted and there was a note of superiority, of holding the winning hand in his voice. "At least all of my girls were willing and legal."

Brent screamed and launched himself at Fred punching him in the ribs. "You know nothing," he screamed into Fred's face.

"I have proof, and if you threaten me again, I will ruin you," Fred said.

"You're dead, you hear me, you're dead," Brent screamed and then turned and walked toward the door.

That was the end of the video. "Do you mind if I send this to my phone?" Lola asked.

Sam shook his head.

"Do you think Brent saw you?" Lola asked, wondering if the boy was in imminent danger.

"Nah, not a chance, I've hidden in that house enough to be able to get out of his way. But it does sound like he killed him."

"Yes, it really does," Lola said. "Did you tell Tyler?"

Sam shrugged and shook his head. "No, I was too scared. I know I should give this video to the police."

"Yes, but I can do that for you if you wish. If you didn't tell Tyler, why did he want you to lie?"

"He's always hated Brent... and Fred for that matter."

Lola asked him some more questions, gradually teasing out the relationship between Fred and his stepson. It was complicated, as was the relationship between Brent and Tyler. Then she asked him about his dog, and he told her something that blew her mind. Lola was excited, part of her wanted to run to Wayne and show him the video, and what she had found out, but she wanted to stay with Sam a little longer. He had been very brave to show her the video and she knew that he was scared.

"Can I drop you at home?" she asked.

"Nah, I can walk but I'll be here at 4.30 on Friday if you happen to be walking Sassy."

"I think that is a good time for a walk, I'll see you then and call me if you need anything or if you remember anything else, any time."

Lola rang Wayne and asked to meet him. While he was happy to do so, he didn't want her to come into the police precinct station. She understood totally. Though nothing he had done had been illegal, he was helping her out, and a lot of police didn't like that. In her mind, a good policeman, or copper, as Tanya always called them, was one that wanted to see justice. Though she didn't believe in breaking the rules and becoming as bad as the criminals, there were times when you had to think creatively.

So, they were meeting in a little coffee shop two streets down from the precinct. The police building had always fascinated her. It was built of what looked like large molded concrete blocks and though she knew it was very old in her mind it still looked modern. In fact, in some ways, it reminded her of home. She wasn't waiting long when Wayne walked in and running a hand through his blond hair, he scanned the room.

Lola was enjoying a cappuccino in the corner and waved him over. "Can I get you a drink?"

"Just a normal coffee would be great."

Lola ordered the drink and explained what she had found out and who she thought the killer was. It took him by surprise, but not as much surprise as she had expected.

"I see your logic," Wayne said. "What evidence do you have?" The smile on his face wasn't smug; in fact, it was a forced smile to cover his disappointment.

"I don't have any, so I think we need to force a confession."

"I think that will be rather tricky... do you have a plan?" Wayne asked as he sipped his coffee.

"If we get all the people together, Brent, Sam, the family, I'm going to play on Sassy being able to sniff out the killer. Maybe, if we push them they could make a mistake?"

Wayne shook his head. "I think it's a great idea but I'm not sure that it will work."

For a moment she thought he was going to leave it at that and that she had failed but then he shook his head.

"I don't see what other choice we have. I will set it up tomorrow afternoon to meet you there. How about 4.30 PM."

"That sounds like a great idea and a good time for justice."

Wayne smiled.

Lola watched Wayne walk away and sat drinking her own coffee. Sassy had been quiet under the table and as she felt Lola's mood drop a little, she stood up and leaned against her leg. "I'm okay," Lola said reaching a hand down to rub the little Frenchie between her ears.

Lola was okay, she knew she had the right person, she just had to find out a way to prove it. Wayne had been right, this was going to be a lot more difficult than she envisioned. They had the video, they had motive, they had means, but they had that on more than one person. Putting this on the right culprit was not going to be easy.

NOTHING TO STOP HIM

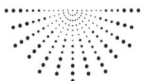

Lola waited around the corner of the Johnsons' house for Wayne to pull up. As he passed her, he gave her a wave and she followed him into the drive. Before he had even gotten out of the car, Brent's car pulled in behind him.

Lola walked up behind the two cars and watched Wayne get out first and then Brent. Wayne looked casual, confident, and in control. Brent looked down his nose a little at Wayne's suit and then raised that nose in the air as he turned toward the house. Then he stopped and turned back. "And who are you?" he asked.

"I'm Detective Wayne Foster, pleased to meet you." Wayne didn't wait for Brent to acknowledge or answer him but turned toward Lola.

"Do you have this all in order?" Wayne asked.

Lola gave him what she hoped was a reassuring smile even though her stomach was turning over and over with nerves and Sassy was leaning against her leg thinking she was going to have an attack.

"Let's get this party started then," Wayne said and walked boldly up to the door.

Wayne did his policeman's knock and the door was answered by Sandra a few seconds later. Her eyes widened and her hand flew to her chest. "How can I help you?" she asked.

"It's okay, Sandra. I promised I would find the killer and I now know who it is," Lola said. "I'm sure you know Detective Foster, we're here to explain it all and to arrest the murderer."

Sandra seemed to sag at the knees but her face remained remarkably composed. There was a hint of moisture in her eyes but she smiled and let them through. "I never did like Brent," she whispered as they entered the kitchen.

Sat at the kitchen table were Sam and Tyler on one side. Lola had rung Sam earlier and asked if he could ensure that Tyler was here. The boy seemed happy to help and had assured her that he could.

Conner was reading a book at the end of the table. The boy still looked so sad and tired. Brent was stood to one side and already drinking coffee from a machine behind the boys.

"I told you to leave my mum alone," Tyler said standing to his feet and rushing across the kitchen until he was right in Lola's face.

Sassy let out a little bark and growled at the boy's ankles. He drew back his foot as if to kick the little dog, but Wayne stepped in between them and shoved him out of the way.

"Quite a temper there, young man," Wayne said.

"And who are you?" Tyler asked his hands on his hips and his shoulders back with eyes wide with rage.

"I'm Detective Wayne Foster; Lola and I have been investigating your father's murder."

Tyler glanced from Wayne to Brent and then to his mum. For a moment he wobbled on the spot and then he raised his head and looked at Brent. "I knew he done it."

Lola watched Sandra cringe at the boy's bad grammar and expected her to say something. Only she didn't.

Wayne touched Lola on the shoulder to remind her of the plan. Swallowing, she took one look around the room before directing her glance at Sandra.

"I'm not sure how much you know about me but I'm a Private Investigator, as is my very well-trained French bulldog. She has been trained to sniff out blood, people, the scent of where someone has been, and she's very good at it. She can tell from a six-month-old fingerprint, who left it and she will find evidence of who committed this crime. If you follow me to the garden, she's going to investigate where we think the murder was committed."

"Don't be stupid," Tyler said. "The dog hasn't even got a nose, how can it smell out anything."

"Well, she is highly trained and she indicated to me that you smoke cannabis," Lola said.

Tyler's mouth dropped open, shocked that he had been caught. However, it soon closed and it was clear that he didn't care. Of course, Sandra wasn't his mother and Brian was his father, why was the boy here and not with his father?

"I'm tired of this," Brent said and turned as if to leave.

Lola looked at Wayne, they had nothing to stop him from leaving.

WHO DONE IT

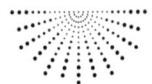

Lola thought that Brent would leave and that they could do nothing to stop him. It was a shame for she needed him here.

Wayne turned. "Brent, we have some video evidence of you attacking Mr. Johnson. There were some quite nasty allegations made on the video, apart from the murder, they are some allegations that we would be very happy to discuss with you down at the station."

For the first time since she'd met him, Lola noticed Brent's confidence was knocked. However, he covered it up quickly and simply smiled. "Of course, I'm always happy to help the plod out."

Wayne grimaced slightly at the insult but smiled at Lola.

Taking a deep breath Lola pointed at the door. Sandra rose and made her way across the kitchen. At first, she thought others wouldn't follow, but Conner went with her; next, Sam went, and then Tyler. Lola followed them with Sassy at her side leaving Brent and Wayne to bring up the rear.

Once outside Lola made her way across to the swim pond. She had forgotten just how beautiful it was, how serene, how peaceful. It was such a shame that it had been marred by such a heinous crime.

Ignoring her audience she pulled Sassy's service harness out of her bag and put it on the dog. She had hoped to get one that said dog detective, but couldn't find one and so this would have to do. She had already spoken to Sassy and told her what the plan was. The little dog would examine the area where Lola thought the murder had taken place, she would then mark a rock, and then go and mark the killer. She marked things by putting her nose very close to them and then barking.

Lola leaned down and rubbed Sassy behind the ears. "Okay, my little sweetie, go do your stuff."

Sassy gave a bark and Lola pointed at the area she wanted her to search. The little Frenchie put her nose down sniffing the rocks working backward and forwards in a way that would cover the complete area. The large round stones were hard for her to walk on and she was scrambling and slipping but all the time she kept sniffing. When she came to the area where the rocks seemed to be out of the perfect placing she stopped.

Lola waited for her to bark, but she didn't; instead, she lifted her head. Lola scanned the people behind her, only one person was smirking. Only one person thought they had got away with murder. Lola had been right in her analysis and for a moment she felt cold.

"Remembering," Sassy said, and then lifting her head she ran away from the pond and toward the house.

Tyler was laughing. "I told you that dog was useless. I bet it couldn't sniff a sausage if you put it on the end of its nose."

"Lola?" Wayne asked.

"I suggest we follow her, she has the scent of something, I just don't know what."

Lola set off to the house and didn't look back to see if anyone was following her. Once inside she could hear

Sassy barking and she made her way through the house toward the sound.

Soon, she was in a corridor, the walls were cream and lined with family photos. Doors lined the corridor and the barking was coming from further down. There was one door toward the end of the corridor door and one on either side and they all looked like bedrooms.

"Hey, get out of there," Tyler shouted and rushed past Lola. "Get that freak of a dog out of my room, now!"

Lola ran into the room to see Sassy sat in front of a chest of drawers, barking.

"I smell blood, did before, faint, didn't recognize it because of funny smoke. Same blood as outside," Sassy said."

"Well done, you are such a special girl," Lola said and she turned to see the rest of them piling into the room.

Tyler ran towards Sassy and the little dog began to bark and growl at him furiously. For a moment Lola thought he would still kick her and she cringed knowing she was too far away to intervene. At the last moment, he shrank back, afraid.

"Tell them, Mum, they have no right to be in my room," Tyler shouted.

Lola turned to Sandra. "My dog has smelt something, I believe it's in that chest of drawers. Do I have your permission to look?"

Tears were running down Sandra's face but she nodded.

"I'm sorry, Mrs. Johnson, I need you to confirm that verbally," Wayne said.

Tyler now looked as if he was going to run from the room but Conner, Sam, and Brent were all blocking the doorway.

"Don't even think about it, kid," Wayne said as he pulled out some gloves and an evidence bag from his pocket. Slowly, he approached the chest of drawers.

Lola called Sassy off and the little Frenchie came and sat beside her. When Tyler tried to move, she growled at him.

Wayne searched the top two drawers and found nothing except for a few bags of cannabis. He pulled open the third drawer and Lola noticed Tyler cringe. Wayne searched in the drawer and pulled out a white towel. It was wrapped around something. Wayne gave her a smile and put the towel on the bed. Slowly, he unwrapped the towel, and as he did it was marked with blood and was holding a blood-covered rock. It was obvious that it was one of the stones from around the pond and that was why there appeared to be a gap. The boy had kept it as a souvenir of his murder.

Lola shuddered, how could he be so cold?

"Do you have anything to say for yourself?" Lola asked.

"I hated him. I hated the man, he was arrogant, mean, and always after somebody younger and prettier. He was making a fool of my mum and I wanted her to be back with my dad. It wasn't really a crime, I just hit him, just so things could go back the way they should be, then he fell in the water."

Wayne stepped forward and grabbed Tyler's right wrist a little bit harshly forcing it behind his back, then he grabbed the other one and handcuffed the young man. He then read him his rights, and nodding to Lola, he dragged him out to the car.

Lola knew that the confession was only the partial truth. They may never know why this happened. Had Tyler lost his temper and then after the first blow he liked what he had done? The body wouldn't have fallen into the pond; it had to be pushed or carried there. It didn't matter, they had a confession. They had enough and she let out a big sigh.

"Why was I here?" Brent asked.

"Mainly, to put Tyler at ease, but also just to let you know that I'm watching you," Lola said.

Brent grunted and turned to leave, not even saying a thing to the grieving widow and her younger son.

Sandra was crying and clinging to Conner. "It's okay, Mum, it will be better now."

Sandra sobbed even harder and pulled him to her. "Yes, my sweet boy, I think it probably will.

Lola left them to it and walked outside to find Sam stood next to her car.

"Thank you for helping me," she said.

"Will Tyler go away?"

Lola nodded. "Yes. I'm sure the rock will test positive for Mr. Johnson's blood; hopefully, there will be DNA from Tyler on it too. If not it doesn't really matter, he confessed and it was found in his bedroom, hidden. You are free of him, make the most of it."

"I intend to. I really found that exciting, I think I want to join the police, so I better get some schoolwork done," Sam said and then shrugged.

"That sounds like a great plan. Why don't I drive you home?"

A NICE SURPRISE AND A NEW CASE

Wayne kept Lola informed about how the case was going. The rock had been tested and there was both blood from Fred and DNA from Tyler on it. He was currently being held in a juvenile facility awaiting trial.

Lola had visited Brian Sharp and Felicity once more. It only occurred to her at the end of the case that Tyler was Brian's son. It hadn't taken him long to confess that both he and Felicity were terrified of the boy.

Felicity believed that he had disposed of her cat. She had no proof, but he had been cruel to him and was very smug when the cat went missing. "I hate to say this, but he's where he belongs. I hope he never gets out," she said before making Lola a cup of tea and giving her some homemade carrot cake.

Lola didn't tell them that the turning point had been Sam telling her that he thought Tyler killed his dog, he only believed it when he found him burying a cat. It was Felicity's cat.

Brian could only agree. As much as he loved his son, he did not want him near him and he knew that Sandra was afraid of the boy too.

With luck, they would both get their way, the evidence was strong against him, Tyler was likely to be locked up for many years.

Lola had completed her purchase of what used to be the garage and had booked some contractors to come in and make it nice for her. Tanya was teasing her about moving, and how she hated her to go, but she knew she was secretly happy for her.

On the work front, she was back to divorce cases. It was both a welcome relief and an annoying reflection of modern life. At least twice a week she met Sam at the park and they walked Sassy together. His schoolwork was coming on great and he looked so much more relaxed now that he was away from Tyler.

Every time they met he talked about his excitement and how he wanted to join the police force. Lola invited him over for an evening meal with Tanya and Wayne. Wayne and Sam got on great and Wayne promised, that if he kept up with his studies, that he would recommend him to the force.

It was a couple of months later and Lola sat with Sassy on her knee all alone in the house. Tanya was out at the gallery as there was an exhibition that night and Wayne had been called back into work. When he got the call, Lola had felt her excitement kick up; of course, she wasn't invited along on the case.

She heard a car pulling into the driveway and shortly afterward Tanya came in.

"I wasn't expecting you back until later," Lola said.

"I'm on a quick break," Tanya said, she looked stunning in a black shift dress with her hair perfectly in place. "I thought you might like to come up to the gallery for a look around?"

Lola looked down at her scruffy jogging bottoms and T-shirt. "I'm hardly dressed for it."

"Come on," Tanya said dragging her from the sofa. Sassy gave a bark and followed them. "Yes, you can come to," Tanya said.

Tanya quickly pulled some clothes out of Lola's wardrobe. There was a pair of black trousers, and a white shirt. "Put these on." While Lola dressed she rooted around for something else and pulled out an old black jacket. It was one Lola hadn't worn for a long while but it was still in good condition and very smart.

Lola donned the jacket, fixed Sassy into her service harness, and followed Tanya out of the house. Once they were in the car, she got curious. "You are up to something?" she said.

"You will see," Tanya said and fixed her eyes on the road in such a way that it brooked no more conversation.

"Okay," Lola said.

The journey to the gallery only took them 10 minutes and they were soon inside. "I really wanted you to see these pictures," Tanya said as she guided Lola across the magnificent room.

It was huge, with marble floors and columns, the walls were painted in cream and lights highlighted the paintings. The place was buzzing with elegantly dressed people oohing and aahing as they walked around and stared at the paintings.

Tanya was rushing across to the other side of the room where a large group of people was admiring some paintings that seemed to have pride of place in the exhibition.

Tanya squeezed them through the crowd and Lola came face-to-face with a painting of the cornfields from the bottom of South-Brooke Hill. The fields were dotted with red poppies that led the eye up the hill, past the houses to the cathedral and the castle. It was a magnificent view and so beautifully depicted that it was even better than a photograph. Lola was never really one for the arts, but this took her breath away. The love and patience that had gone into this picture were astonishing and the crowd obviously agreed. It was priced at £2000 which seemed a lot in some ways and not enough in others.

As they continued to watch, the price was changed to sold. A slim dark-haired man in his mid-20s nodded at Tanya as he placed a sold sign over the price and then walked away.

"You should see this one too," Tanya said and guided Lola past other pictures equally amazing. There was one of the cathedral in the daytime, one of it at night, there was a picture of the memorial at bomber command. Lola hadn't visited this yet but she intended to do so. It was a 31-meter-high sphere of rusted steel that sat on a hill some miles away but with a view of the cathedral. The spire was surrounded by rusted metal walls containing the names of 57,861 men and women who gave their lives to support Bomber Command in WWII. Once more poppies could be seen in the distance and the view through the memorial to the cathedral was stunning. The sky was dark, menacing, and Lola found the painting haunting.

Tanya stopped and Lola nearly bumped into her.

"What do you think of this one?" Tanya asked.

Lola turned to find a magnificent painting of Sassy staring back at her. The painting depicted the little dog perfectly. You could even see the cheekiness in her eyes. Lola felt her mouth drop open as all she could do was stare.

As she regained a little of her composure she looked to the place where the price should be and was disappointed when it said that the painting was not for sale.

"Would you like to meet the artist?" Tanya asked.

"Y.. y...yes," Lola managed.

"Turn around," Tanya said and the twinkle in her eyes was unmistakable, she was having fun.

Lola turned around to see Louisa Meek standing before her with a massive smile on her face. The one-time PA looked so different. She was dressed in black trousers and a red top that sashayed around her hips and looked both smart and fashionable. With only a touch of makeup and her hair in a high ponytail, she looked younger and so much more relaxed. Before Lola could say anything Louisa threw herself into Lola's arms and hugged her tight.

"I can't thank you enough, you believed in me, and you introduced me to Tanya, I can't tell you how much my life has changed and how fabulous this is," Louisa garbled her words as she pulled away.

"These are all yours?" Lola asked. Though she sounded astonished, in many ways she wasn't, she had seen the talent that Louisa had previously.

Louisa nodded. "This one is new, most of the rest I had already done. But some of them are new."

"They are fabulous and I would love one like this of Sassy."

Hearing her name Sassy gave a little bark.

"That's why it's not for sale," Louisa said. "This is the one I did for you and I want it to be a gift."

"I couldn't accept it, it must have taken you hours," Lola said. "I want it, don't get me wrong, I have to have it, but I agreed to pay and I want to pay."

"You can argue about the cost of it later," Tanya said. "Let's go have a coffee, we can talk more up there."

Upstairs there was a café that was serving drinks and cakes and light snacks. Tanya got their order while Lola and Louisa chatted.

"How are you doing?" Lola asked.

Louisa smiled and clapped her hands together. "This is my biggest dream come true. Tanya has made me a permanent exhibitor here and my paintings are selling well. After this, even Tanya wants me to increase the price and we have a business plan being made up. I should never need to work again and I have you to thank for all of it."

"No, I just introduced you to a friend, the talent is all yours. I still want the painting of the cathedral but if you sell it do me one from the garage, showing my new business, and then up to the cathedral and I insist on paying."

"I will do that, it sounds like a great idea. Maybe I should put you and Sassy in the foreground, small, so you have to look for you? I think it would be fun."

"I would love that," Lola said. "I am paying. I have a trust fund. I have never used any of it for my parents died while I was deployed. They never wanted me to enlist so I felt guilty. I know they would be overjoyed to have me spend some of the money on those two paintings."

Tanya arrived with three cappuccinos and three pieces of chocolate cake.

"Okay, I accept," Louisa said, "but I still owe you."

Louisa, Lola, and Tanya stayed at the gallery until late. After a while, Lola and Sassy went and sat in a corner, with Sassy curled up on her knee. Lola pulled out her phone and opened her kindle app and began to read.

"Well, long time no see," a man's voice said.

Lola looked up and was surprised to see a handsome man with neat brown hair spiked to perfection and intense blue eyes. Roger Ellis. He was a local reporter and she had gone on a couple of dates with him when she first arrived in England. She found out he had been moved to Manchester so they lost touch.

"What are you doing here?" she asked and then shook her head. "Sorry, that sounded rude."

"Mind if I sit?" he asked.

Lola shrugged. "Be my guest."

"I'm back in Lincoln... for a few months anyway. Do you want a coffee sometime?"

"I'm okay for a coffee, but I don't think I want a relationship just yet," Lola said. She liked Roger but he was a reporter and she didn't want to get involved with a man who may soon be gone.

"Okay," he said just as Tanya arrived.

"The Gallery's closing, Roger, if you can make your way out," Tanya said.

Lola noticed that it was darker and that most people had left.

Roger agreed, "I'll call you."

* * *

Lola was driving as Tanya looked exhausted. She had been at the gallery since 5 am and it was now gone midnight. As they turned down the hill into the village the garage was on the right. Lola slowed to look at the property, the work was coming on well. Out of the corner of her eyes, she spotted a van and three men and slowed the car.

"What is it?" Tanya asked.

"There are people there, what are they doing?"

Tanya lifted her phone and took a series of pictures and then she rang Wayne. Lola had pulled over just past the garage and was getting out of the car.

"Wait," Tanya called and put her hand on Lola's arm. "Wayne is sending a car, it will be here any minute."

Lola sat back down and heard Sassy growl beside her. "I know," she said. "I want to chase them off too."

Tanya laughed. "I swear you talk to that dog as if she understands you."

Lola shrugged just as they heard the police sirens approaching. The sound of doors slamming was followed by the roar of an engine and a rusty white transit van pulled out and drove away.

Lola started the car.

"No, we should wait," Tanya said.

Lola could see she was afraid and so she decided to wait.

The police arrived and one car set off in pursuit but Lola doubted they would find anything. Where the roads led there were no cameras and plenty of side roads for them to disappear down.

Lola and Tanya joined the officers on the large open driveway that used to be the garage forecourt. Wayne arrived just as they got there.

On the ground were a jackhammer and shovels. The men had dug up the tarmac and were starting to dig up the ground.

"What is this about?" one of the officers asked Wayne.

"I don't know lads but I guess we'd better see what they were after."

"Oh-oh," Sassy said. "I know what that smell was, from before."

Lola had an idea she knew too. What had she gotten herself into?

To find out what Sassy can smell, Grab The Bulldog and the Buried Body now.

THE CASE OF THE MIX-UP MURDER

ALSO BY ROSIE SAMS

Join Rosie's Newsletter here for all the latest on her books and occasional FREE content.

The Art of Murder

Murder Afoot

Mai Tais & Murder

Grab The Bakers and Bulldog Mysteries now. 20 sweet cozy mysteries with Smudge, Melody, and all the gang for just 0.99 or even better FREE with Kindle Unlimited.

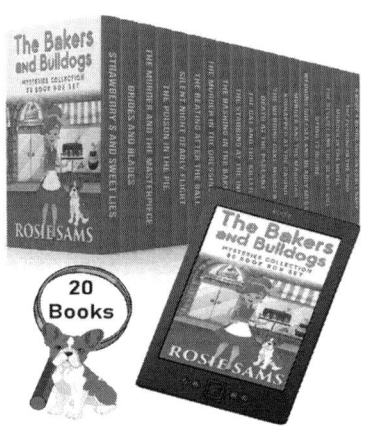

To be the first to find out when Rosie releases a new book and to hear about other sweet romance authors join the exclusive SweetBookHub readers club here.

***

If you enjoyed this book, Rosie and Lila would appreciate it if you left a review on Amazon or Goodreads. This picture is a hint about their next book.

©Copyright 2021 Rosie Sams
All Rights Reserved
Rosie Sams

License Notes
This Book is licensed for personal enjoyment only. It may not be resold. Your continued respect for author's rights is appreciated.

This story is a work of fiction; any resemblance to people is purely coincidence. All places, names, events, businesses, etc. are used in a fictional manner. All characters are from the imagination of the author.

Printed in Dunstable, United Kingdom